TRACKS

Maria Grosskettler

Gabriella & Winnifred,
May your Tracks take you to beautiful places.
Maria Grosskettler

Tracks

Copyright © November 5, 2020, by Maria Grosskettler

www.mariagrosskettler.com

All rights reserved. No part of this publication may be reproduced, distributed, or transmitted in any form or by any means, including photocopying, recording, or other electronic or mechanical methods, without the prior written permission of the publisher, except in the case of brief quotations embodied in critical reviews and certain other noncommercial uses permitted by copyright law.

This book is a work of fiction. Any references to historical events, real people, or real places are used fictitiously. Names, characters, places, and events are products of the author's imagination.

ISBN: 9781735948102 (paperback)

Library of Congress Control Number: 2020920321 (paperback)

Cover Design: Josh Merow

www.joshmerow.com

For Everett, may your love of books continue to grow as you grow.

Prologue

Monday, June 22

THE LOS ANGELES NEWS
Remembering Addison West

By Grayson Guilfoyle

The death of actress Addison West hit Hollywood harder than a flopped ten-million-dollar budget movie. Last week, the nation and the world were stunned by the unexpected death of this entertainment icon. Over the weekend, thousands of adoring fans and hundreds of national and international celebrities gathered in Colony Beach outside of Los Angeles to attend her memorial service, which was a special tribute to a remarkable woman and her extraordinary life.

Ms. West's son, up-and-coming film producer Ryan West, eulogized his mother by recounting the well-known accomplishments of her public career. Upon her death at the relatively young age of sixty, Addison West will best be remembered as a charismatic star and winner of multiple Oscar, Emmy, Tony, and Grammy awards. She was also a philanthropist for countless service projects, including the Addison West Foundation, supporting single parents.

Little, however, has ever been known of Addison West's personal history. As dazzling as she was to the public eye, Ms. West was much quieter about her private life. Throughout her career, West had artfully dodged all personally prying questions, and no such intimate glimpse of his mother was offered by Ryan West in his stoic speech where he never shed a tear. Perhaps even he knows little of his mother beyond her fame.

As we mourn the loss of this beloved actress, we are all left to wonder, *who really was Addison West?*

Chapter 1

Sitting at 315 Jefferson Street in the small town of Berlin, Maryland, just nine miles from the Atlantic Ocean, was a house that fit the very definition of haunted.

Large vines snaked their way around the two-story Victorian style home, leaving barely a speck of the original 1940's yellow paint to be seen. Rotten wooden shutters hung off the siding from rusted-out nails. The roof was missing not a few but half of its shingles, replaced simply by black tarps nailed down. The windows were caked with years of filth and neglect, blocking any light from entering. Even on the sunniest of summer days, the house at 315 Jefferson Street was bleak and filled with gloom.

Mitch Harrison, newly appointed town mayor, stood at the far end of the cracked sidewalk and squinted up at the house in the early morning June sun. He shifted his weight back and forth between his feet and after what seemed like an eternity, took one deep breath, and moved forward toward the house. He stepped over the two rotting front porch steps to stand on the brick porch that somehow still stood firm. With a heavy breath, he lifted his arm against the weight of gravity and uncertainty and knocked on the front door.

Inside, a man peered through the cloudy haze of dust and sunlight to a grandfather clock. Thirty minutes past eight in the morning. Then the man squinted his eyes into the kitchen where a calendar hung on the wall - Sunday, the 25th of June.

Another knock echoed through the stillness of the house.

The man took a deep breath like a bull getting ready to charge on its matador and yelled, "Who is it?!"

His voice sliced through the air and sounded as unfamiliar to him as it did to the man knocking. With another, even more painful puff from his chest, he added, "And what do you want?!"

The angry voice of Crazy Ernie split the ears of Mayor Harrison as if each word were really a knife. He still had time to make a run for it. He had heard the stories all his life. There was still a missing woman from sixty years ago and the only link to explain her disappearance was this man.

But Mayor Harrison knew this visit was essential if he wanted to save his town. And he knew he couldn't put it off any longer.

He only now wished he had told someone.

The Mayor took a deep breath and nervously replied, "Mitch Harrison." He waited. When no response came, he added, "Newly elected town mayor."

Like another set of knives came the angry voice of the town's still suspected murderer. "I don't care about any town politics! Get out of here!"

Mayor Harrison took a deep breath. "My visit is not for political reasons. I… I…" He leaned closer into the door and whispered, "I've come to ask about the train station on Old Route 50."

The man whom all the townspeople called Crazy Ernie stood in his entryway and could not believe he had just heard those words. He never thought he'd hear that name again before his dying day. He leaned one hand on his cane and wiped a bead of sweat off his forehead with the other. "What's it to you?" he sneered through pierced lips.

Mayor Harrison did not hesitate this time. "The town has a great opportunity that I'd like to discuss with you. It will only take a moment of your time."

There was silence.

Then came the sound of a slow and steady creak as if the house's bones were finally moving after sitting for too long.

Mayor Harrison held his breath.

The creaking stopped and a loud, sharp click of a deadbolt forced the Mayor to take a step back from the door. The weathered knob turned, and a ray of light pierced into the tomb of the house, illuminating the wrinkled face of Crazy Ernie.

"You have five minutes and then you're out!" Ernie snapped and turned back to the living room.

Mayor Harrison followed behind the man into the darkened room but left the door cracked behind him, just in case.

One yellow incandescent lightbulb cast an eerie glow across the hazy living room that smelled like mildew blended with cinnamon. On the side nearest the front door sat a piano that was covered in newspapers and, to Mayor Harrison's astonishment, *gossip* magazines.

The middle-aged man stepped closer to examine the hundreds of *U.S. Weekly's, Star's, Extra's,* and *TMZ's*. The top layer of magazines were all dated within the past month. He would have expected to see this in a teenage girl's room, but not a man in his eighties. Just as the Mayor reached down to read the headlines of the most recent *Star,* Crazy Ernie barked from across the room, "Well, what do you want?!"

Mayor Harrison's fingers snapped up to his chest.

"Yes, yes, of course, sir. As you know, the station has not been used in years, and we have an offer from some folks from out of town that they want to…"

"It's not for sale!" barked Ernie, cutting the Mayor off.

"They aren't looking to buy it. They just want to…" Mayor Harrison tried to step deeper into the room, but Crazy Ernie threw his cane into the air, stopping him.

"I don't give a dog's bone about no folks from out of town! That building is mine! No offer of any kind will change that!"

"But sir, you see…" Mayor Harrison staggered back toward the piano. His hand landed on its edge.

"You leave that place alone! You hear me!"

It was in that moment of disappointment that Mayor Harrison glanced down at where his right hand had landed to the headline of a newspaper, *Remembering Addison West*. Even Mayor Harrison knew of the death of Hollywood's most famous actress, so it wasn't the headline that drew his eyes closer to the paper. It was the newspaper's name that intrigued him - *The Los Angeles News.*

How did a man who never left his house come across a black and white printed newspaper from 3,000 miles away? the Mayor thought.

"That's it?! That's all you came for?!" shouted Ernie. The mayor was too confused to respond. Ernie stood and growled, "Get out of my house now!"

The Mayor snapped back to reality. "Please, sir," he pleaded. "Reconsider this. The town needs this chance!"

Ernie raised his cane to just inches from the Mayor's neck. "I know all about you, Mitch Harrison! You may be the new Mayor, but it was your father and his father before him who ran this town into the ground! Losing all its hard-earned money! You better not ever find yourself back in this house asking for any sort of help to bail you out of your inherited mess! You hear me?!" The man grew an inch with each increasingly anger-filled word, drawing his cane closer to the Mayor's throat.

Mayor Harrison cowered back toward the entryway, but as he did so, his elbow knocked a small item off the edge of the piano. When the object hit the ground, it popped open, and a soft child's lullaby broke the tension-filled room.

Crazy Ernie waved his cane in the air. "Turn that thing off and get out of my house!"

Mayor Harrison sidestepped around the music box toward the entrance and slid out into the safety of the sunlight.

The music continued to play on the stale air of the house at 315 Jefferson Street.

Chapter 2

Later that evening, twelve-year-old Natalie Carpenter sat with her feet dangling twenty feet above the train station on Old Route 50. She stared down at the stark black roof. The building was a perfect rectangle from her angle. When her brother had picked this tree to build their treehouse, she didn't understand why.

"We can watch all the people coming and going in and out of town on the trains. We can hear all their stories and soak up all their adventures!" Natalie recalled him saying as he nailed the first board for the ladder into the trunk of the tree.

Half of those wooden boards were now missing or broken, and she and her brother never even finished building the walls or the roof. And a train never did roll through that station. No passengers. No luggage. No stories. It had been abandoned all of Natalie's life and who knows how many years before that.

Natalie stared down at the train tracks and wished for her brother's vivid imagination to picture her own life when she could finally escape Berlin. Her chin rested on the makeshift railing, and her brown-haired curls fell off each side of her sunburned shoulders. In the distance, the summer sun had finally set behind the tree line that ran along the edge of the cornfield turning everything in its path gold as if the land itself was the most priceless treasure in the world.

This was her cue to head back home. She swung her legs up and around to rest on the five-by-five-foot platform that served as the floorboard to the treehouse. She reached for her backpack at the exact moment when a black SUV peeled down Old Route 50 and made a beeline into the train station's gravel lot, spewing up a cloud of dust. Natalie paused to wait until the driver made its U-turn to head back to the beach, but the engine suddenly clicked off, and the first visitors she had ever seen to that old train station stepped out of the car.

Even though Natalie was certain no one could see her with the angle of the sun, she rolled over onto her belly and peered over the edge. One of the men was tall with a tight-fitting gray suit over a muscular frame. The other man was the complete opposite with short stature and an oversized black suit to cover up his belly that popped out over his belt line. This man wiped his forehead with the sleeve of his jacket as he coughed through a cloud of dust, "This the place?"

The taller and much younger man stared at the train station. "Yes," he said as a smile spread across his face.

"Ha!" coughed the other man, "Looked better in the pictures!"

The tall man slipped his phone out from this jacket's inside pocket and swiped it a few times. "This is the address listed, and if Google Maps are up to date, then we are exactly where we need to be."

"Well, it better be worth it!"

Each of the men pulled out small notepads from their jackets and began to walk around and stare at the outdated building, occasionally looking down to take notes.

The younger man placed a hand on the siding and held it there. "I can't believe it's real," he said in a whisper, but somehow the wind caught the words and carried them to Natalie's ears as she squinted her eyes to try and get a better look at who he was.

The short man rounded the corner to meet him. "You know? If this whole thing flops, I'm putting it all on you." His chuckle pierced the air like a firecracker on the fourth of July.

The younger man peeled his hand off the siding and reached up to pull down some vines from the nearest window frame. He whispered something to himself and then dusted off his hands and turned to stare down the tracks that disappeared in the distance to the west. He gave a faint smile and then turned back to his partner, "We should be going. You ready?"

The shorter man was already leaning against the car. "Yeah! More than ready. Let's go find a drink."

The younger man met him at the car but he turned and took one last look at the building before getting in. Then he slid into the front seat, closed the door, and just as fast as they had arrived, Berlin's newest visitors were gone again, stirring up the dust that had just begun to settle.

Natalie had spent her whole life in Berlin, and no one had ever cared about that old train station, so why now? She scrambled down the wooden planks but had forgotten which were broken and landed on one with such force that she caused the wood to split in two. She fell backward to the ground, landing on the palms of her hands. Two sharp stings zapped right up to her elbows, but there was no time to process the pain as the SUV was already back on the road and heading out of sight.

As quickly as she had hit the ground, Natalie popped up and sprinted into town, knowing exactly where the men were headed.

Chapter 3

"Watch out!" shouted a voice as Natalie's body slammed onto the pavement at the intersection of William and Pitts Streets.

Her vision was slightly blurred as she rolled onto her front and lifted herself off the ground. "You should be the one to watch out! What the heck do you think you're doing?" she said to a boy about her age who had already stood up and was picking up the books and clothes that had fallen out of a box.

"You ran into me," he said.

Natalie didn't have a second to argue with him. She rolled her eyes and with one huff, she headed on her way to the alley behind Pitts Street.

The boy shouted, "Wait! Where are you going?"

Natalie heard his footsteps following behind her as she turned down a darkening alley but didn't bother to glance back. Her foot was already on the fire escape ladder that hung down from a second-story landing when the boy shouted again, "What are you doing?!"

Natalie turned around and snapped her finger to her lips, "Shh… Go away! Why are you even following me?" She continued her climb up but the boy was quick on her heels. At the top of the landing, she flung herself around to face the boy who hung just a few feet below on the ladder. "Seriously! Leave me alone!"

The boy staggered back just enough to allow Natalie to return to her task at hand. She spun on her heels toward the small storage door, but when she pushed down on the handle, she found that it was locked. *That's odd,* she thought. Natalie had visited this room countless times with her brother when her dad used to work at Burley Oak Brewing, and this door was never locked. She wiggled and pulled, trying to jar it loose.

"Looks like you could use some help," said the boy from behind her. Natalie jumped at his voice. In her panic, she hadn't even heard him step up to the platform.

"Listen, you have to leave me alone!"

"Fine, fine," the boy said, taking a step back as he lifted his arms halfway in the air. "I'm just curious how you plan on getting in?" He had a smug look on his face.

Natalie glared at him and returned to pulling at the handle. But still, nothing. She turned back and stared at the boy whose straight sandy-blonde hair hung in front of his green eyes. He wore a V-necked gray-blue shirt with one pocket on the chest and a pair of khaki shorts. He had on ankle-high white socks and a pair of Vans Slip-Ons. "And I suppose *you* know how to get in?" Natalie scoffed.

"I can try," said the boy, using his hand to toss his bangs to the side. He squeezed past Natalie and squatted down in front of the lock to examine it. Natalie watched as he pulled out a tiny screwdriver from his pocket, lifted it to the door lock, and with a few wiggles and turns, she heard a click.

Natalie clapped her hands together. "Thanks!" she said, and she disappeared through the door and into the darkness.

Chapter 4

John Paul Waters had no idea why he decided to follow this strange girl into a pitch-black room, nor why he had assisted in an actual break-in! It was his first day in a new town. The town his mom had sent him to stay *out* of trouble for the summer!

He wasn't proud of the series of events that led him to spend his days off school away from his friends, even though they were half the reason for it. It wasn't that he ever intended to get into trouble but just like this moment, he often found himself in the wrong place at the wrong time. And his curiosity always got the best of him.

He stepped on a beam inside an old storage space and waited a moment for his eyes to adjust to the darkness. He could just make out the shape of the girl on the other side of the room, so he put one foot in front of the other to cross the beam to reach her.

On the other side of the room, the girl opened a door and a small ray of light cut through the darkness, making John Paul's last few steps much more manageable. Then the girl took a seat on one side of the doorway and stared up at John Paul. "You're starting to annoy me." But as she said it, she motioned for John Paul to take a seat opposite her.

He did, but the doorway was so narrow that their bent knees touched. "I'm Natalie," the girl said, holding out a hand.

"John Paul," he replied, accepting the shake. "So, what exactly are you doing?"

Natalie squinted her eyes. "Spying…" she said. "What are you doing in Berlin, by the way?"

John Paul knew that her question must have been related to the reason she was spying, but the truth was that he had debated how to respond to that question for three weeks. He couldn't outright say the real reason he was there, but he also didn't want to fall into a web of lies because he had learned in his twelve years that lying never gets you anywhere. You just have to stretch the truth a little.

"Visiting my aunt for the summer while my mom finishes up some classes," he said.

Natalie nodded. "Who's your aunt?"

"Emily Hope."

"Oh! She was my fifth-grade teacher last year!" Natalie exclaimed in excitement. "I had no idea she even had a nephew!"

"Yeah, my family is not that close."

"That's a bummer. Ms. Hope is awesome."

"Yeah, she seems pretty cool so far," John Paul said. "Plus, she got me a job working at the hotel with her for the summer so I can make some extra money."

"Oh, yeah, I forgot she works at The Atlantic when school is out. Don't know how she does it with all the ghosts hanging around."

"Ghosts?" John Paul asked.

"Ghosts!" confirmed Natalie. "That place is haunted! Every floor has a different ghost roaming around, always tormenting the staff and the guests."

John Paul tried not to laugh at how serious she was being. "Like how?"

"Just little things to the staff like messing up beds when no one is in the room or moving cleaning supplies. They bother the guests worse. Taking their keys or clothes. Turning the water to freezing cold or scalding hot when they are in the shower. Opening the window when it is raining or snowing. All sorts of stuff!"

John Paul couldn't help it anymore and he let out a laugh.

"I'm serious!" said Natalie, but at that moment, she peered out farther into the hallway and added, "Sh… Stop talking!"

John Paul leaned out farther too, but when he couldn't make sense of what she was listening to, he asked, "So who are we spying on?"

Natalie pulled herself back to the door frame and went on to tell him about the two men who arrived at some old train station.

John Paul was confused about why she seemed so interested but kept nodding along with her as she spoke.

"So, I think that's them that I hear!" she said at the end of her story.

This time, they both leaned out into the hallway to listen.

A man's voice became clearer. "That's right! This town is a guaranteed gold mine!"

"A gold mine?" John Paul asked.

Natalie shook her head. "I don't think they're talking about an actual gold mine, but something about using our town to make money like a gold mine, which is straight crazy because there's no way to make money in this town! Even the people living here are having a hard enough time with that. My own dad has been in and out of four jobs in the past year!"

Music began to play louder and the voices of the two visitors became fainter. "I can't hear a thing. I'm going to get closer," Natalie said, and she slid into the hallway and tiptoed down the set of stairs. John Paul took one deep breath and followed.

There was a small bar storage area with kegs of beer and crates stacked high with aluminum cans at the bottom of the steps. Natalie leaned around the corner. John Paul was up a few steps and held onto the wall to do the same. For a Sunday night, the bar was packed. Two men in suits sat at a nearby table with another man wearing a bright pink polo shirt.

"And I told you, gentleman, there is just that one little kink in our whole plan," said the man in the pink shirt.

"That's Mayor Harrison," whispered Natalie to John Paul.

"We know, we know," said the plump man, "But we will take care of that."

Mayor Harrison took a sip of his drink and continued, "I don't know. He seems pretty set on never letting anyone touch that train station. Don't know why. There's nothing special about it."

A person rounded the corner in front of the stairs carrying an empty keg. Natalie slid back a step, but as soon as the man dropped the empty keg next to the others, he spun around and spotted them on the stairs.

"What in the name of?!" the man stammered. "What are you two doing in here?"

John Paul grabbed Natalie's arm and the two sprinted back up the stairs, through the doorway, across the beam, and onto the platform. Natalie slammed the landing door shut and slid down the ladder, jumping off mid-way and landing on the pavement with a thud.

"Let's go!" she shouted up to John Paul.

John Paul attempted to move just as fast as she had but after the third rung down, his right foot got stuck on the rusty rail. Between the pull of gravity and his rushing momentum, John Paul fell off the ladder, falling five feet to the ground. His hands hit the pavement first. With a heavy breath, he looked up and watched as this girl he had just met disappeared into the shadows. Then he heard the door above open and someone shout something down at him. Without a glance upward, he used his bleeding hands to push off from the starting line and sprinted into the darkness.

Chapter 5

After they cleared the downtown area and made it to a row of houses, Natalie slowed her pace. "Finally!" John Paul said, out of breath. He hunched over and put his burning hands on his knees.

"Sorry. Last thing I want is to get caught spying. You'll learn soon enough that everyone knows everything in this town!"

"Well, that guy never even attempted to follow us so I think we're safe."

The two passed the sign for Stephen Decatur Park as Natalie led the way to an old dinosaur play structure. She sat down on its head and started picking off more of the already chipped green paint. John Paul found a spot on the dinosaur's front foot to sit.

"What is it with some old train station, anyway?" he asked.

"I have no idea!" exclaimed Natalie. "It has been abandoned for as long as I can remember so it's really weird to have people just show up out of nowhere asking about it. The only people that come to this town are the ones looking for a quick bite or to buy some dumb antique, and then they all head right on to the beach."

"Well, that's not the case for me," John Paul said.

Natalie smiled at him. "That's true…" She continued to stare at him with an awkward smile.

"Why are you looking at me like that?" John Paul asked.

Natalie jumped up off the dinosaur's head and used it as a footrest. "Because there's only one place folks can stay in town!"

John Paul stared at her. "At the Atlantic Hotel?"

"You guessed it!" said Natalie. "So, I'm super grateful you decided to be annoying and follow me tonight because now you can be my inside-man!" She slapped him on the shoulder. "Do you start work tomorrow?"

"No, I'm just going in with my aunt in the morning for a tour and for her to tell me some things. I don't officially start until Tuesday."

"Well, perfect! I will meet you at the hotel tomorrow and we will make a plan!" She held out her hand.

John Paul looked from Natalie's face to her outstretched hand. He had promised his mom he'd stay out of trouble for once in his life.

But what harm could come from a little eavesdropping. He threw out his hand and said, "Deal!"

@news_in_gray

Grayson Guilfoyle
Reporter of the stars for The Los Angeles News

After the success of her most recent blockbuster, Juliette Charles isn't planning on taking a break. "I'm ready for the next great film! Who has it? Bring on the Oscar nominations!"

Chapter 6

The following morning, John Paul walked alongside his aunt Em to The Atlantic Hotel. Everything in Berlin seemed within walking distance, which was new to him. Where he lived, neighborhoods were clustered together and all the shops, hotels, and restaurants were a fifteen-minute drive without traffic. Berlin was definitely small-town America.

For the next few weeks, his work location was a three-story tall building with more than two dozen windows just lining its front, along with a large porch filled with plants and rocking chairs. There were a small gravel drive and a green picket fence that separated the hotel from Main Street. It truly looked like something out of an old movie. He was shocked to find out that it was a hotel and not a museum.

As he and his aunt climbed the two brick steps to the porch, John Paul rubbed his hands. His aunt held the front door open for him and then led the way to the left where a small room was set up as a reception area. She made her way around the desk and dropped behind it as John Paul took a seat at one of the wooden chairs under the window and stared down at his hands.

After returning home from the park, he had spent nearly fifteen minutes scrubbing his palms clean. He had plucked out tiny bits of pebbles from the open wounds, but as he stared at them now, he knew he had only gotten half of them.

His aunt popped back up from behind the desk. "We will wait for Mrs. Fritz to arrive to talk you through what your responsibilities will be, but I can give you a quick tour of the hotel if you'd like."

John Paul nodded and shoved his hands into the pockets of his cargo shorts.

Aunt Em led the way from the reception area back into the front lobby, but it was unlike any lobby of a hotel he'd ever seen. It was more like the entry to a house. A large chandelier hung from the ceiling. Hung on the walls were a variety of old-fashioned photos. A large wooden staircase lined with a red carpet was on the right side of the room. Just before the stairs, there was a doorway that was closed off with a metal gate.

"That's the Drummer's Cafe. It doesn't open until 11:00 for lunch so I will introduce you to the staff later. In there," she pointed to a room on the opposite side, "is the room we use for large group gatherings like weddings and such, or it can function as a conference room if needed."

From where they stood, John Paul could see through the set of five windows and door straight into a large room which appeared mostly empty except for a few tables lining the wall, a large banquet table in the middle that had no chairs, and on the far end was a fireplace with a few chairs and a coffee table.

"And that leads you right back into the reception," Aunt Em indicated another doorway in the banquet room. "Let's head upstairs and I'll show you some guest rooms."

Aunt Em led the way up the long flight of stairs to the second-floor landing. At the top were two doors that led out to a balcony. "Guests can come in through the front or up these back stairs, but this door only opens with a room key."

John Paul followed her around the stairs to the long hall of guest rooms.

"All rooms have a particular name. You will learn them soon enough once you start cleaning. I'll let you peek in a few as we go by, though some are occupied."

Aunt Em started to the left and past the next flight of stairs that led to the third floor. She showed John Paul The Rose Room, The Byron, The Elizabeth, and The Blue Room. All had the look as if an old woman lived in each. *No wonder this place is haunted,* John Paul thought to himself.

"Excuse me, ma'am," came a voice from down the hall.

Aunt Em glanced over to the woman and said, "I'll be right with you." Then she turned to John Paul, "Just wait here. I shouldn't be long." Aunt Em quickly walked the hallway's length to the other end where a woman stood with the door cracked open.

John Paul was prepared to wait until she returned, but he heard a screen door open and saw two familiar-looking men step out onto the porch. He glanced back up the hall and saw his aunt follow the woman into her room. Without thinking, John Paul rushed past the steps and moved his body against the wall to the small, partially cracked window next to the door. He had a clear view onto the porch and even out of suits, he recognized the two men from the bar from the night before.

Chapter 7

Natalie woke up earlier than usual and for the first time in over a year, she was excited about what the day might bring. After grabbing a quick breakfast, she snuck out the backdoor of her house, cut through the lawn past her dad's work shed, and took the back alley straight into town, just as she had done time and time again with her brother.

As the homes gave way to buildings, Natalie arrived just in time to see her small sleepy town come to life. Residents were heading to their jobs at the various shops and restaurants that somehow still remained in business. There were only two customers inside the coffee shop. The mailman was just coming out of the post office with a box full of envelopes.

It was a typical morning in Berlin. Except for one thing.

At every business and street corner, Natalie overheard the conversations that all included the question of, "Who those men are?"

When she reached the corner of Bay Street and Main, she found Mrs. Peters standing outside her antique shop with her hands glued to her hips as she stared down Mr. Cole across the street. "I'm telling you, Robert; they are here from the State. They are probably looking to fine us for tax evasion. No one has been able to maintain this town's finances in years! We've surely gone bankrupt and that silly Mayor of ours never even told us!"

"Not a chance!" retorted Mr. Cole. "I bet they are just passing by on the way to the shore and figured they'd stop in for a drink. You need to quit running water through the rumor mill, Susan."

The two continued to bicker as Mr. Brushmiller walked across the street to add in, "I was working at the brewery last night and I saw them talking to the Mayor. I'm pretty sure they said something about the Atlantic, so I think they stayed the night."

Natalie picked up her pace and tried to avoid eye contact, but Mrs. Peters shouted her name five seconds after she had passed the Town Center Antiques. She stopped in her tracks, took a deep breath, and spun around.

"You hear anything about those two men who popped into town last night?" Mrs. Peters asked as her eyes narrowed in on Natalie as if trying to suck out any secrets she might be hiding. "Some say they checked in at The Atlantic."

"No, I haven't heard anything," Natalie said. She bit the inside of her lip. Mrs. Peters' eyes narrowed a little more and Natalie felt the secrets begin to inch their way out of the deepest part of her belly as if being pulled by some invisible string that was being cast out of Mrs. Peters' piercing blue eyes.

"You sure? I know you and your br... I know you are always running around town. You sure you haven't heard anything?"

"No," Natalie said, shaking her head. "I was just on my way to check out some books at the library."

"Well, aren't you—,"

But before she could get the rest of her sentence out, Mr. Levinski came strolling across the street, pulled a toothpick from his lips, and said, "Did you hear about those rich folks wanting to buy our town? And who the heck are they showing up on Sunday night?"

His mustache appeared to move in anger with his mouth. It kept twitching even after he finished speaking as if a fly was tickling the top of his lip and the mustache itself was trying to shoo it away.

Natalie peeled her eyes off the caterpillar sized lump of hair and leaped at the distraction to slyly sneak away around Rayne's Reef Restaurant.

As she rounded the corner, she spotted something moving around the tires at Wainwright's. It was larger than a cat but just as skinny as the barn ones from the Webb's farm. It paced between the trash cans on the side of Wainwright's Tire, sniffing frivolously as it went. Natalie immediately recognized the black dog as one of the rescues her mom had recently placed in a new home. Puzzled where its owner was, Natalie bent down low and held out her hand to try and draw the dog to her.

"Pah, pah, pah," she tutted, piercing her lips to do so and working to extend the sound of the letter P. When that didn't get his attention, she tried T. "Tah, tah, tah…"

The dog didn't budge from its mission, so Natalie inched closer. She lifted one leg forward making an arc before gently placing it back on the ground, like how a chameleon moves.

A loud clang of metal on asphalt from inside the garage distracted the dog from its sniffing. He looked up, making eye contact with Natalie, and then darted across the street and through the parking lot behind The Globe restaurant.

Natalie leaped out of her crouch and chased after it. The dog kept to a straight line but took a sudden sharp turn under a wooden fence between The Globe and The Atlantic Hotel. Natalie skidded to a stop and dropped to the ground. The space was far too narrow for her to slide through. She watched the dog make its way toward the row of homes on Jefferson Street.

A loud creak from above startled Natalie up off the ground. She looked up to the hotel's balcony and saw the screen door open and two familiar-looking men step out into the morning sunlight. She quickly slid behind a row of bushes to keep out of sight.

Chapter 8

"I think she'll love it," said a hoarse voice from above that Natalie recognized as the short man from last night.

"I sure hope so," said the other, smoother voice of the taller man. "It was a lot to convince her to fly across the country all the way from California to a town she's never even heard of."

"It's a part of the job description, kid."

"Yeah, I guess so," said the other man, still sounding unsure.

"It'll be fine. And she'll only be here for two weeks max." The railing screeched as the man who was talking leaned over it, just above Natalie's head. A strong cigarette smell wafted down with the wind and she inhaled more than she wished. She covered her mouth and tried not to cough.

The younger voice said, "We just have a lot to get done in a little amount of time."

"Ah, that's what the crew is for! They will be arriving soon and will fix everything up the way we need it," said the man with the scratchy voice.

"If the town will even let us. You heard what Mitch said last night."

"Listen, the Mayor told you it would be fine, and you said you know a way to take care of that problem with the old guy, so I'm not sure what you are so worried about," said the man through a puff of a cigarette.

"You have no idea..." The younger man's voice trailed off.

"Listen, I know this is your first big rodeo, but just think, when all is finished here, we will be rolling in dough." Natalie heard a slap and could only assume Mr. Cigarette's hand had found its way to the other man's back. "Let's get to work."

The door opened again with a creak. "I just have to make a quick stop first," said the younger man.

Natalie waited until she was sure they weren't returning to the balcony and slid out from behind the bushes. She crept along the outside windows of the Drummer's Cafe and headed to the hotel's front entrance. She carefully opened the door and peered inside. The coast was clear, so she stepped into the foyer. As she walked toward the staircase, a raspy voice from behind shouted, "What are you doing here?!"

Natalie spun on her heels as Mrs. Fritz's tiny stature marched up to her, hands clinging to her hips.

"Well, what are you doing here?" she repeated.

Natalie hesitated, "I was looking for Ms. Hope's nephew. We said we were meeting here this morning."

Whatever Mrs. Fritz lacked in vertical space, she made up for in a strict demeanor. "They are busy with a guest at the moment! Wait out front. We have important business to attend to here and don't need any more distractions!"

She hurried Natalie along to the front door, but a loud bang thundered down from the second floor, forcing Mrs. Fritz to spin around.

"Go!" she shouted, giving Natalie one more push on the back before sprinting up the stairs.

Natalie began to walk out the front door when a hand suddenly wrapped around her arm and pulled. "C'mon! The guy went this way!"

Chapter 9

Ryan West had no idea how the events since his mother's death had led to the spot where he now stood. At the end of a cracked sidewalk that led to a dilapidated house. In one hand, Ryan West held a silver object and in the other hand was a ticket stub with only a departure station listed.

The heat of the mid-Atlantic summer sun was already beginning to course its way through the layers of atmosphere and even at nine in the morning, a drop of sweat materialized on his forehead. He wiped it off with his forearm. It wasn't even the heat of this place that was so bothersome. Ryan West had lived in southern California his whole life and knew a thing or two about summer days, but since arriving in Maryland, he found it difficult to breathe in the thick fog of humidity that made the 90 degree days feel like 110! He longed for the Pacific Ocean breeze.

Ryan West took one, long deep breath before finally deciding to walk up to the front door. He paused at the steps and looked down at them. They were both rotten out. He lifted his head back to the door but instead of moving onto the porch, he turned around.

This is ridiculous, he thought.

As he walked back to the street, a familiar song began to ring in his ears. He had listened to that song as many times in the past two weeks as he had his whole first few years of life. It was hard to get the melody out of his head and he took this as a sign that he was where he needed to be. He turned around again and headed to the door.

At that exact moment, Ryan West heard a screech.

"Who's there?" came the raspy voice of an old man from within the shadows of the house.

Ryan's body became rigid. He had thought long and hard about what he would say but, at that moment, all he could muster was, "Sorry to bother you, sir."

"Are you the one messin' with my dog? You leave him alone, you hear!" the old man was out of view in the shadows. "I don't want anyone comin' round this place no more!"

Ryan didn't attempt to move closer to see the man's face. He let the angry, old man continue his rant about people having no respect these days and how he just wanted to be left alone.

The muscles in Ryan's face all seemed to lose their structure as if gravity began to pull at them just a little harder. His eyes lowered to the ground and then his head followed. Without another word, he robotically turned his body and walked away, leaving the man's voice to trail off between the growing space that separated them.

@news_in_gray

Grayson Guilfoyle
Reporter of the stars for The Los Angeles News

The rumors are true!!! Ryan West, son of Addison West, has been spotted in Berlin, Maryland! Just weeks after he spoke at his mother's funeral, Ryan West was seen across the country in some no-name town with none other than Guy Barnes himself!

Chapter 10

Once the tall man was out of view and the old man had closed his front door, Natalie and John Paul leaped from behind the bushes where they were hiding and sprinted up Jefferson Street to where the train tracks met the road.

Natalie followed them in the direction to her treehouse, taking long strides over the graveled rocks to land only on the wooden ballasts. After a few minutes, John Paul said from behind, "I think we can slow down now!"

Natalie fought against the rushing blood in her veins and pulled her legs back into a walk like pulling the reins on a horse.

John Paul caught up to her and then stepped up to a rail to try and balance. He huffed the question, "What the heck was that all about?"

"I have absolutely no idea!" Natalie admitted, shaking her head, and deciding to fall in sync with John Paul on the opposite rail. Her mind hadn't stopped racing since he had grabbed her arm and dragged her out of the hotel to spy on the bizarre interaction between the two strangers.

"Well, who was that crazy old dude that lived in the house?" John Paul asked.

"Crazy Ernie," Natalie responded matter-of-factly. "And I have no idea what that guy would want with him! The man stays locked up in his house. I've never actually seen him or even heard his voice before! I've only ever heard the stories…"

"What kind of stories?" asked John Paul.

Natalie thought back to the ghost stories her brother and his friends used to tell her. Some of them were so scary that she purposely avoided walking anywhere near 315 Jefferson Street. The worst one was about a little girl, but she couldn't even bring herself to share that one aloud.

"All sorts of stories," she answered. "Like that his skin has turned white because he hasn't been in the sun for sixty years, or that he eats any kid who walks on his lawn!" She jumped off the rail and headed across the train station platform to her treehouse.

"Those can't be true!" John Paul exclaimed as he followed Natalie.

"Maybe not," said Natalie, placing her foot on the first rung of the ladder. "But the whole town knows he was involved in the disappearance of his wife. It was just… no one ever could ever prove it."

"What do you mean, *disappearance?*" John Paul asked.

"Vanished," said Natalie as she reached the top and pushed up the trap door to the treehouse. She looked down at John Paul on her heels. "One day she was here and the next, she wasn't. No one ever saw her again."

"What do people think happened?"

Natalie took a seat in the middle of the platform and crossed her legs. Once John Paul made it through the narrow opening that served as a trap door, he did the same.

Natalie looked him straight in the eyes and said, "Some say that he *murdered* her."

Just as those words rolled off her lips, a black SUV pulled into the parking lot of the train station causing both Natalie and John Paul to jump. Natalie's heart skipped into overdrive as she held her breath and dropped to the floor of the treehouse, pulling John Paul down by the shoulder to do the same.

They leaned over the edge and watched as the tall man they had just spied on stepped out of the car. He pulled off his sunglasses and looked around a full 360 degrees. Then he walked toward the front door.

"What's he doing?" Natalie whispered to John Paul.

"I think he's going to…" but before he could finish his sentence, the man pulled a silver key from his chest pocket. He walked to the front of the building and out of view.

Natalie looked over at John Paul who looked back at her.

"Let's just wait here," John Paul said. "We don't know how long he will be so we can't risk him seeing us."

Natalie was good with that plan, but the few minutes of waiting felt like an eternity. Finally, the man emerged from the front of the building, walked to his car, stepped in, and drove away.

"Let's go check it out!" said Natalie.

As the two rounded the front of the building, they found the door locked. "Great," John Paul said.

"Can't you just pick the lock like you did yesterday?" asked Natalie.

"Nah. I don't have that tiny screwdriver with me. It was just in my pocket from fixing my mom's sunglasses earlier that day."

"Dang. I guess let's try and find another way in."

John Paul nodded. "I'll go this way," he said and headed to the right.

Natalie took a step back to get a better view of the train station. After months of hiding out in her unfinished treehouse, she never really took that much notice of the place but as she observed it now, it didn't look in that bad of shape. It was covered in standard horizontal siding and still had all its roofing shingles. There were two windows on the front, one on each side of the entrance door. Natalie moved to the left and tried to pry one open, but it was sealed shut.

She rounded the corner and checked out another window. Locked. As she peeled her hands off the window ledge, she spotted another window that was higher up. Next to the window was an old storage shed. Natalie eyed up the height and headed to the edge of the train station's platform. She turned around and clicked her heels together like a gymnast.

Then she sprinted.

When she reached the shed, she took one giant leap and clapped her hands to the top. With her feet kicking wildly, she pulled herself up. She crawled over to the window and pulled off some vines, revealing that it was cracked open.

"John Paul!" she attempted to whisper shout, but he was already turning the corner. "It's open!" She gestured to the window and then moved closer and slid her fingers under the worn wood. With all the might she had, she pushed up. It moved a few more inches until… *Creak!*

The window jerked to a sudden stop and wouldn't budge any further. Natalie stared at the slim opening. It would be a tight squeeze. She sucked in her belly and pulled her hands over her head to dive in. The top half of her slid in easily, but the bottom half got stuck. Her stomach rested on the windowsill with a pinch. "A little help here!" she shouted.

She heard a thump and then felt her ankles lift in the air as John Paul pushed her in. As soon as her hips cleared the opening, she fell forward. John Paul squeezed her ankles tighter just as her hands smacked the floor.

"You ok?" he asked.

"Yeah. Just toss my feet in. I'll try and catch myself."

It didn't work out as she planned, and Natalie's bottom half came faster than she had expected, and she pummeled into a heap on the hard, black-and-white tiled floor of a restroom. "You still ok?" John Paul asked, peering in through the crack.

"Yeah, I'm good. Meet me at the front door."

After Natalie unlocked the door for John Paul, she began to explore the space which looked more like an abandoned museum. Historic artifacts were scattered on tables and desks. Everything from eyeglasses to a pocket watch to a set of men's cufflinks. It was as if someone had purchased the last ticket out of town and left everything else to fade with time.

She stepped closer to a desk to examine the items when John Paul said from across the room, "Check this out."

He was standing in front of an open safe mounted into the wall. "Do you think this is what that guy came for?"

Natalie peered inside. It was small and probably used as a safe box for any money the station had before they could get it to the bank. She ran her hand along the inside and felt an indentation on the bottom of the safe. When she pulled her hand out, it was covered in dust and cobwebs. "I don't think so," Natalie said, showing her hand to John Paul. She wiped off the filth on her pant leg and then went to touch the strange indentation again. It was a figure 8, and inside each circle was another indentation. Natalie stood on her tippy toes to look in. "A" was in one circle, and "P" was in the other. She figured that must be the safe company's logo.

She shrugged her shoulders and dropped down off her toes. "Yeah, this thing has been empty for years."

Natalie made her way back to a desk on the other side of the room and began to explore. She opened drawers and looked for any clue as to what that man was doing. With no luck, she walked over to a podium that sat in the middle of the room. A large book was left open to the last page. It was filled with narrow rows and columns of cursive writing. Natalie lifted the leather cover to look for a title but there wasn't one. She dropped the cover back down and noticed that it wasn't the very last page she was looking at. The actual last page had been torn out. She flipped around the pages before, trying to figure out what was significant about the missing page but after leafing through the book a few times, it appeared that every page was the same.

Almost.

The tiny rows were broken into columns. At the top of each column for every page had the following words: Passenger, Cargo, Weight, Date, Time of Departure, Time of Arrival, Station Operator.

Suddenly, one name jumped off the page like a cricket jumping up from high grass and hitting her leg with a sting. Under the column for Station Operator for more than a dozen pages was Frank E. Price.

Pages upon pages of Frank E. Price's signature signing off on the comings and goings of the trains. The initials were the largest and each had swooping lines to make the signature more elegant. Natalie touched the name with her finger and ran it down the rows and rows of the same signature. A chill ran down Natalie's spine like the one you get when the water from the shower hasn't warmed up enough. She felt the hairs grow on her arms and legs.

Chapter 11

"Who is Frank E. Price?" John Paul asked. He had watched Natalie's finger run down the rows with that name.

She rubbed both of her arms and said, "Just another ghost story."

John Paul couldn't believe the number of ghost stories one town could hold, but he let Natalie continue.

"Frank Price had owned the train company and was so money-hungry that he forced all of his employees to work around the clock, even kids as young as six! One night, a worker became so fed up that he lit the train station on fire. Being so obsessed with money, Frank Price risked his life to get the trains moving north before the fire reached them, but it was too late. Everything burned to the ground, including Frank Price…" Natalie continued to stare at the book. "Story has it that his ghost rides on a train across all the old rail lines on the shore looking for revenge."

John Paul didn't believe a word of it. "Well, clearly, that's just some old ghost story because we are standing in the train station and the guy's name is written right there."

"I know! It doesn't make any sense! Where did the story come from?"

John Paul couldn't answer that question. He honestly had no idea what all this was about and part of him felt guilty about getting mixed up in it all. Really guilty. He thought back to the promise he had made to his mom. He needed to find a way to tell Natalie he couldn't help anymore.

But before he could think of an excuse to abandon the mission, the sound of tires on gravel broke the silence. Natalie rushed over to the window and peered out.

"Hide!" she whispered. John Paul glanced around. There weren't many places to hide in the room. Natalie ran into another room and waved her arm as she said, "This way!"

John Paul followed. There was a small door in the far corner of the room. Natalie sprinted to it and pulled it open just as the car engine shut off.

"Hurry!" she said.

John Paul skipped into the closet, which was small and had a musty smell. He carefully closed the door behind him. Inside the cramped space, John Paul could feel Natalie's breath on his neck. It reminded him of playing hide-and-go-seek as a little kid. After a brief silence, he heard footsteps outside as a shadow crossed through the ray of light shining beneath the door. John Paul held his breath and could tell from the lack of movement next to him that Natalie had done the same.

A high-pitched ring caused Natalie to push closer into him and he had to steady himself not to fall. Another ring followed but was cut off by a familiar voice. "This is Mr. West."

There was a pause as the person on the other end of the call spoke.

"Today? But we don't even know if we can even start shooting."

A pause.

"Ok, ok, I'll be there. And you're right; there's plenty of good places elsewhere in town while we wait."

Another pause.

"I know, I know. It has something to do with that Price guy but I'm still figuring that part out. Listen, I'll meet you there."

John Paul suddenly felt the urge to itch his back. He twisted his shoulder blades back and forth, praying it was just an itch and nothing else. All he wanted to do was burst out of the closet, but suddenly the sound of music filled the air. The melody sounded like something you would play to help a baby fall asleep. It faded in and out of earshot.

Then the phone rang again. The music ceased and the man named Mr. West answered the ring. "I'm coming!"

Chapter 12

"So somehow that West guy knows about that Price guy?" John Paul said to Natalie as they left the train station. He was once again pulled by curiosity to stay on the case.

"Seems so," said Natalie, staring at the ground. "I wonder if he ripped that last page out of that book."

"What would he need with some page from some old book... from some old place?" John Paul said, waving his hands in the air.

Natalie rolled her eyes at his choice of words. "That's just it - I have absolutely no idea! Frank Price has always just been a ghost story, and that train station has been abandoned all my life!"

"And have you lived here all your life?" John Paul asked her.

"Yeah, my parents moved here when my sister was three. She's seventeen now. My brother and I were born here." Natalie stopped talking as it somehow felt weird mentioning her brother to John Paul. She didn't want him to ask questions, but then it dawned on her how much her brother would have loved this adventure.

And how much John Paul reminded her of him.

The two walked in silence until John Paul finally asked, "So, where are we going now?"

After leaving the station, Natalie didn't have a plan. She thought about her brother again and what he would have done. He was always the one to come up with the good ideas. Or not-so-good ideas. Either way, he still found a way to convince Natalie to execute whatever plan he had. Anything from stealing a chicken from the Webb's farm just for fun to diving into the creek at midnight for an old pocketknife. Her brother thought of something and she did it. Natalie rubbed the pocket of her backpack where she kept that knife and tried to think like her brother.

As if the knife had magical powers, an idea popped into her head. "I know exactly where we should go!"

She sprinted between the houses to reach Main Street.

The Calvin B. Taylor House Museum was a three-story home that stood at the corner of Main and Baker Streets. It wasn't a long distance to cover on foot from the train station, but Natalie wanted to be there as soon as it opened.

Once she reached the driveway that faced Baker Street, she cut a beeline across the museum's side lawn and jumped up onto the front step, nearly taking out one of the potting plants. The front door was partially cracked open, and Natalie could see Ms.

Taylor's long torso wrapped up with her typical waist sash around a floor-length dress. Even though she had no relation to the Taylor family who had lived there, Ms. Taylor took her role in preserving history very seriously.

"The house remains one of the town's greatest accomplishments," she said to a group of three visitors who must have arrived early. "It would have been demolished and turned into a parking lot if our town's Historical Society hadn't stepped in. We do everything we can to preserve all the historic buildings in the town."

She opened the door fully and was about to take a step right into Natalie but stopped short and exclaimed, "Well, hello, Natalie. What brings you to the museum today?"

"I just had a quick history question I was hoping you could help me with."

Ms. Taylor smiled. "Let me finish up with these visitors. Why don't you wait in the dining area?"

She opened her arm and like an arrow pointing the way, directed Natalie and John Paul into the house. The entire home was decorated in beautiful, multi-colored fabrics: the carpets, the chairs, the window curtains, and even the wallpaper. Natalie's fifth-grade class had taken the official tour just this past school year and she had learned that all of this was a display of the Taylor family's wealth back in the 1800s. Natalie ran her hand over the velvet rope that separated visitors from the pathway and the dining set. She began to imagine a family sitting at the table enjoying a meal. She couldn't recall the last time her family all sat down together to eat. That was mostly her fault, but she found it easier to be away from them.

"What can I help you with?" Ms. Taylor asked, causing Natalie to spin around to face her. "And who, may I ask, is this?"

"This is John Paul. He's Ms. Hope's nephew," said Natalie.

"Oh, I hadn't realized Emily had a nephew."

John Paul chuckled, and Natalie smiled. "Yeah, that seems to be the trend."

Ms. Taylor gave a puzzled look, but Natalie continued, "I was actually looking for some information about the railway history. I know you were collecting items for a new exhibit, so I wanted to check with you."

"Oh goodness, we have gotten so much in about the railways!" Ms. Taylor said, clapping her hands together in front of her mouth. "I plan to hopefully make a whole museum just for it! I am having quite the time sorting through the boxes, but I can't say no if someone wants to donate something. Follow me. I'll show you what I have." She led the way up the narrow staircase.

Chapter 13

The first room at the top of the stairs was made up to look like an old-fashioned child's room. A crocheted blanket lay across the bed and small porcelain dolls with painted faces sat in tiny little chairs placed underneath the window as if a child had just finished playing with them. Across the hall was another room set up to look like the master bedroom with a fireplace, complete with an antique fire screen that Natalie had learned was used to reduce the discomfort of excessive heat.

Ms. Taylor continued past these two rooms and into a third room, which was set up like an office with a large desk in the middle. On the right wall were photos of the famous horses Man-O-War, War Admiral, and Seabiscuit.

From here, Ms. Taylor led the way into the back storage room. It was filled with boxes, papers, and random antiques from women's dresses on mannequins to milk jugs and crates to even old-fashioned turn signals. The place was an Eastern Shore historian's treasure trove.

On the wall nearest Natalie was the start of a museum exhibit on the railway. Old photographs of passengers hung on the walls. Natalie stared into their faces. Even in black and white, she could see a sparkling of hope in their eyes. The dates below each photo were a timeline, showing the first trains that rode through this part of the world and the people so eager to ride from the bay to the ocean. As Natalie followed along the walls, taking in their stories, more photographs revealed that it wasn't just people who moved on the tracks but produce, oysters and other goods.

"Sorry about the mess," said Ms. Taylor. "We have been a little short-staffed here at the museum and there aren't too many willing volunteers to sort through all this. Especially in this heat." She wiped a drop of sweat off her eyebrow before she began to move some boxes around.

Natalie tiptoed around a pair of antique candlesticks lying on the floor.

"I do remember seeing a set of books that might help… " Ms. Taylor said, as she immersed herself in a box of papers. After shuffling through the top half of the documents, she stood up, put her hands on her hips, and looked around. "Let me check over here."

She moved to the far corner of the room, leaving the box she was just looking through still open with papers and photographs scattered on the floor around it. Natalie began to return the documents to the box when a black and white photograph caught her eye. It was of a train station like the one she was just in. In the photo was a group of men all in fancy suits and holding briefcases.

"Ms. Taylor, do you know anything about this photo?" asked Natalie, holding it up.

Ms. Taylor popped her head out from behind a wall partition that was being used to display information about peaches. She squinted at the photo. "That one? Oh, those are the Drummers."

"The Drummers?" Natalie asked.

"Salesmen. The original come-here's in my opinion. You have the from-here's and the come-here's. They were a part of some of the first come-here's. They were called the Drummers back then because they would come from the big cities of Philadelphia and New York drumming their sales pitches to anyone who had at least one good ear to listen." She stepped back behind the partition.

"What were they selling?" asked John Paul.

"Oh, anything and everything. Just trying to make a dollar from our poor citizens. Most of the stuff was just gimmicks. Anything from elixirs to cure gout or make you live longer to the newest technology like stopwatches and even washing machines! That railway was the only way the Industrial Revolution made its way to our shores. We would probably all have English accents without it and the changes it brought."

She returned from behind the partition with a cardboard box. "I knew I had it somewhere."

"Why did the trains stop running?" Natalie asked as Ms. Taylor propped the box on a table near the window and began to rip off the tape.

"Many reasons, I suppose. Here in Berlin, it had to do with some family problems…" She trailed off as she began to flip through the books. "Was there something particular you were looking for about the railroad?"

"I just wanted to find out about a family name I came across. *Price*. I think that it is somehow connected to the railway." Ms. Taylor glanced up from the books and narrowed her gaze, but quickly returned her eyes to search in the box.

"If it's railways you are interested in, you really should make a visit down to Queponco Station in Snow Hill. It was turned into a museum not too long ago. I know Mr. Pullman would love to show you around. He's helping me try and do the same thing… Oh, here is one that might help!" She popped her head out of a box and handed Natalie a book entitled *Eastern Shore Railroad*.

The cover was sepia-toned and had a photograph of train cars on a barge in the water. Natalie quickly flipped through the pages as Ms. Taylor reorganized the box.

"Was there anything else you needed?" she asked. "I have a meeting I need to prepare for."

Questions zoomed around Natalie's head but she couldn't piece together words that would make sense to anyone else, so she just said, "No, not right now. Thank you for this."

"Of course, and try to visit Mr. Pullman down in Queponco."

"Yeah, for sure," said John Paul.

Sunday, December 28, 1959

BAY AREA GAZETTE

Berlin Train Station Comes Down in Flames

By Robert Paxton

What police suspect as an electrical problem brought down the train station on Jefferson Street in downtown Berlin late last night. Firefighters responded to a call from Joseph Fritz at approximately 11:30 p.m. By the time they had arrived, there wasn't much they could do to save it. "We just had to contain it," said the fire chief, Gary Yards. "We were glad it didn't spread to the neighboring homes."

Frank Price, owner and operator of the Eastern Shore Railway, watched from his front porch as his business burned to the ground. "We were just lucky no one was hurt," was his only comment.

Chapter 14

"Where did you find this?!" snapped Natalie, snatching the newspaper clipping out of John Paul's hands.

"It was in a box filled with all these old newspaper articles. I tried to find more about the fire, but this cut off clip was all there was," he said.

Natalie quickly skimmed the portion of the article John Paul had found. "You should have asked to take it," she said, suddenly feeling bad.

"I was about to, but did you see how Ms. Taylor got all suspicious when you mentioned the Price name?"

Natalie had noticed but didn't think much of it. John Paul continued, "I just didn't want her to ask questions; that's all."

"That makes sense," Natalie said. She hadn't meant to make him feel bad about it. "But nothing in this scrap of newspaper makes any sense!"

"I thought the same thing at first, but look," John Paul pointed to the article, "It says here that the fire burned down a station on Jefferson Street."

Natalie looked at the article again, realizing she had read over that part. "You're right! So, part of the story is true. There was a fire, but not at the station by my treehouse. But either way, Frank didn't even die in the fire."

"Maybe there was another Frank Price," John Paul said.

Before Natalie could respond, a flash of black bolted across Main Street, followed immediately by a flash of white that Natalie recognized as Mrs. Branson's large poodle, and following behind that was Mrs. Branson herself!

Natalie broke into a sprint.

The flash of black turned out to be that same dog she had seen early that morning. The two dogs barked and ran through the promenade in front of The Atlantic Hotel while Mrs. Branson pulled on the leash of her pedigree-approved poodle.

Natalie watched as the black dog and the poodle caused a domino effect of chaos, sending people jumping out of the way as they weaved in and out of a sea of legs. Mr. Brushmiller popped himself right on top of a trash bin to avoid being knocked over!

"Gosh darn it! Get those dogs under control!" shouted Mayor Harrison, who had just come out of the barbershop with a smock still around his neck and shaving cream on his face.

Natalie anticipated the stray dog's next move and went left around the fence and lampposts in front of the hotel. At the end of the driveway circle for the hotel, the dog made a sharp turn past the barbershop. The poodle wasn't ready for the sudden maneuver and pummeled right into Mayor Harrison, knocking him into a flowerpot that was already decorated for the fourth of July with red, white, and blue pansies. Mr. Hyland snatched Mrs. Branson by the arm just before she tumbled on top of the pile of human and dog limbs.

The black dog headed straight in Natalie's direction, so she crouched low and got ready for the blow but just before the collision, a sharp whistle pierced the air and the dog's ears perked up as he skidded to a stop just feet away from her. He then made a sharp left, out of her reach and down the alley behind the hotel. Natalie stood up and dusted the loose gravel off her knees, disappointed in her second failed attempt to capture the dog.

The streets were a tangled mess of people and objects. Natalie hadn't even noticed the guests leaving the hotel whose bags now littered the promenade. A small lady with white hair frantically picked up her undergarments and shoved them back into a suitcase. Outside the diner, Mrs. Yardley was collecting groceries that had rolled into the street.

Mr. Abbott was helping pat dirt off Mayor Harrison's pant leg. Mrs. Branson was scolding her poodle, who sat on the curb with its head down. All the shop owners were pouring into the streets, carrying with them not just distraught over the dogs but also about the suspicious strangers who arrived last night. Murmurs quickly turned to raised voices as the crowd began to get frustrated.

"This is not the place, Mrs. Peters," said Mayor Harrison, who still had shaving cream on his jawline.

"Not the place?!" she shouted back at him. "It's public property. We can discuss anything we want here."

"I just meant that there are things we need to talk about as a board before we can answer any questions."

"Fine, you go meet with your little folks and we will stay here and chat," piped in Mrs. Yardley, who seemed to have gotten over the fact that half her fruit and vegetables had just been bruised.

Mr. Cole bellowed, "There's no reason we can't talk about it right here and now!"

Everyone started yelling and pointing fists at each other. Natalie could have sworn Mrs. Peters was about to punch the Mayor square in the face if he got any closer. Natalie pulled John Paul up onto a nearby bench to get out of the crossfire.

Suddenly, a loud horn blew through the air causing people to cover their ears and search wildly around for its source.

Mrs. Fritz stormed across the street, air horn at the ready. "This is not the place for such childish behavior!" The Mayor was about to say something, but she immediately cut him off. "Mayor, as a member of the Town Board, I am calling for an official Town Hall Meeting tonight! All of you can come with questions then, but for now, I must insist that you disperse from my hotel's lawn."

Like children being scolded by their parents, all the townspeople began to scatter. Mrs. Fritz pivoted on her toes and walked back toward the hotel, but before she reached the front door, Natalie spotted a vehicle heading down Main Street, but it wasn't just any car.

It was a long, black, shiny limousine, and Natalie wasn't the only one to notice it. The silence soon turned to whispers as the limo headed straight for the hotel's front-drive. There was little that Mrs. Fritz could do at this point to avoid attention to her newest guest arriving.

Natalie thought her town's streets were too narrow for a limo to navigate through, but it pulled onto the graveled drive with ease and came to a stop. The driver was the first to exit. He was thin and tall. He wore a black suit and placed an even blacker hat on his head, looking like a modern-day Abe Lincoln.

The man walked around the back of the limo, indifferent to the crowd of confounded stares pouring over him. He opened the back door, and a large pink sun umbrella popped open. Natalie watched as a woman's purple painted nails wrapped around the shaft of the umbrella, and then, as if being lifted by a string, she gracefully rose out of the back seat. The woman's long, brown hair fell magically down over a golden yellow dress. She tilted the umbrella, blocking the view of her back, and then glided into the hotel.

Chapter 15

Ryan West stared into the full-length mirror and adjusted his tie. It was way too hot and humid to even be wearing a tie, but he knew this meeting was necessary. He walked over to the dresser and opened his bag. He pulled out a large envelope and dropped a key back inside. He was still amazed that it worked to open the train station. It had only been a hunch since he first found it and read the letter, but even after stepping inside the building, he was nowhere closer to understanding what it meant to him.

He slid the envelope back into his bag just as someone called his name from the hall. In his haste, Ryan West hadn't noticed that he knocked a small, silver object off the dresser. With its rounded edges, the item rolled under the bed just as Ryan West closed the hotel door behind him.

⁂

"The old man won't budge! We've been trying to add that property into Berlin's Historical Society for years!" exclaimed Ms. Taylor from across the table that was decorated for afternoon tea. "Why do you think he will change his mind to allow some folks from out of town to come and do whatever the heck they want with it?"

Ryan West took a deep breath as he watched the last of his ice cubes melt into the glass of lemonade Ms. Taylor had given him when they first sat down at the table in the backroom of the Calvin B. Taylor House Museum.

"There has to be something he wants! Everyone wants something," said Guy Barnes. The man leaned back in his chair and folded his hands behind his head. Ryan knew he was lucky to be working alongside him, but with each passing day since he first Google searched 'Berlin, Maryland,' he wasn't quite sure why.

"He's a recluse!" explained Mayor Harrison. "Stays cooped up in that house and never comes out to see the light of day for anything! I tried to talk to him about this, but he wants nothing to do with it!"

"What if we just do it anyway! Come on! This is the opportunity of a lifetime!" said Guy Barnes as he slammed his hands on the table.

The room went silent.

"Is it even necessary?" asked Mayor Harrison calmly, caressing his freshly shaven face. "Can't you just build something in California and make it work?"

Ryan knew that would come up. He had known it all along, but Guy Barnes was nothing but relentless when he found something he wanted. He was the most power and money-hungry man in the business, and he would never back down once he set out on a mission. The minute he saw the train station, Guy Barnes wanted to use it for his next project.

But that was not the reason Ryan West had typed those two words into a Google search box.

As Guy Barnes went on his elaborate explanation as to why the train station was essential, Ryan's thoughts drifted back to that day in his Los Angeles office.

He had spent hours going over all the items his mom had left him; the letter, the ticket stub, the key, the box. None of it made any sense to him, especially since he had never even heard of the town Berlin! It just so happened that the moment he decided to Google 'Berlin, Maryland' was the same moment he had heard a voice from the hall shout, "You found it!"

Ryan had spun his chair around to discover Guy Barnes staring at his computer screen. "Found what?" he had asked him.

"The location for the next project."

Ryan wanted to keep his personal and work life separate, just like he had learned from his mom, but Guy was right. Looking at the images, he knew that Berlin would be the perfect place for the job, but it's been far from the original trip he had in mind.

"What do you think, Mr. West?" asked Mayor Harrison. Ryan blinked his eyes, bringing his mind back to the present.

"I'm sorry, what was the question?" he asked.

"Do you think she will come to the town meeting with us this evening?"

Ryan had missed most of the conversation in his daydream, but he knew who they were talking about. "Yes, absolutely! She lives for those types of things."

"Perfect! Let's start there and we will work out this whole train station thing another day," said Mayor Harrison.

Ms. Taylor scoffed as she pushed her chair back from the table. "This is absolutely ridiculous! I have tried for years to get that building under the town's historic registrar!"

Mayor Harrison waved a hand in the air. "And we have made no progress, Katherine. Maybe this is exactly what we all need. A distraction. Maybe it will prompt that old man out of his house for once and we can make some progress."

Ryan had to chuckle to himself at the Mayor's use of the word distraction. That's what this whole thing was for him. He needed to buy some time to figure out what all the items from his mom meant, and he secretly hoped that they led to more inheritance than just the contents of that envelope.

He pushed back his chair from the table and was about to say his thanks and goodbyes when Guy Barnes said, "Ms. Taylor, do you mind if we speak in private for a moment?"

Ms. Taylor gave him a glare that could have burned a hole straight through the teacup she held in her hand. After a moment, the fire in her eyes simmered, and she reluctantly said, "Fine."

Chapter 16

Berlin's Town Hall sat on the triangular corner of Bay and William Streets. Its doors faced toward Main Street, so Natalie found an open spot on the side of the building next to the Historical Society plaque to wait for John Paul.

She finally spotted him through the crowd, walking with Ms. Hope. Natalie waved them over and the three joined the long line entering Town Hall. Once inside, Natalie began craning her head above the crowd in search of empty seats.

"This way!" Natalie pulled John Paul by the arm through the sea of people, causing him to lose his aunt in the process. The two squeezed into two empty seats near the front just as Mayor Harrison stepped up to the podium.

"Ladies and gentlemen," he bellowed into the microphone. "Attention, ladies and gentlemen!" he said.

Slowly the voices turned to whispers and then dulled altogether. Natalie glanced around and watched as all the townsfolk took their seats.

Mayor Harrison cleared his throat. "I want to thank all of you for changing your evening plans to attend tonight's meeting. I'd like to address some concerns about the new traffic light on…"

"Come on, Mitch! You all know why we are here!" shouted someone from the crowd, not making light of the Mayor's attempt at a joke.

"Ok, ok. Let's go ahead and get on with it. As you all know, we have some new visitors to the town. And for whatever reason, their presence has created a bit of a problem."

Shouts ensued.

"Tell us what they want!"

"That's because of their fancy suits!"

"We heard they want to buy our town! Can they even do that?"

Mayor Harrison raised his hands in a request for silence. "They do want something from us, but to most of your amazement, they just want to simply *use* our town. Just borrow it for a short while."

Fists flew in the air and the shouting grew so loud that Natalie could barely make sense of what people were saying.

"Nonsense!"

"Never in a million years!"

"That's just the beginning!"

"What next?!"

"Let me finish!" Mayor Harrison shouted. "For once, will you people finally be open to the fact that there is a world outside of our little town and that maybe, just *maybe*, people beyond our town are *decent* people. And maybe, just *maybe*, they hope to help our town." His jaw continued to move in anger even after he paused to take a breath.

"We don't need their petty help!" yelled Mrs. Peters.

"Maybe you don't *need* it, but you will want to hear what they'd like to offer to us." Mayor Harrison pounded his fist on the podium and then motioned to the slightly ajar side door that led to the individual offices of Town Hall. The door swung open and two men walked out on stage.

Natalie felt the whole room hold its breath.

The men walked up to Mayor Harrison and each took their turn to shake his hand and pat him on the arm. The man Natalie nicknamed Mr. Cigarette stepped up to the microphone first.

"As Mayor Harrison stated, I also want to thank you all for coming here this evening. I know my partner and I have caused quite the fuss, but I assure you that what I am about to offer is well worth our visit." He eyed the crowd and when no one engaged him with a negative remark or rebuttal, he continued. "My partner, Ryan West, had come across Berlin, Maryland while searching online for historically preserved towns. Looking through those photographs, there was one thing that stood out to both of us."

"Just get to the point!" someone finally exclaimed, breaking the breathless silence of the crowd.

"That is the point. You see, there are very few towns that we come across that are like yours. And though it is something you have never noticed, it is something that is very important in our line of work. You see, your downtown is completely free of power lines." At this statement, Natalie sent a puzzled look to John Paul. Then, like the lighting of a match, there was an outbreak of laughter.

"Power lines?" Mr. Brushmiller asked, holding his belly in glee.

"Yes," Mr. Cigarette pressed on. He had to speak louder into the microphone to explain more. "You can stand at the center of Main Street and look North, South, East, and West and no power lines are blocking your view! Berlin's Main Street has a clear vanishing point in every direction."

Natalie knew this and she guessed that everyone who lived in Berlin all their life also knew this, but why did that make Berlin special?

"I know what you all are thinking," continued the man. "*So what?* From what I have observed in the past 24 hours is that most of you have never actually left this town and therefore, you probably have never realized how truly unique that little fact makes you."

A woman in the crowd finally spoke up. "So, you're saying power lines is the point?"

"Yes, well. The fact that there aren't any, as that is extremely important in our line of work. Let me explain," the man said, picking up the microphone to walk around the stage. "Ryan West and I, Guy Barnes, work for West Coast Studios, directing and producing movies."

Many people gasped at the announcement of his name which meant nothing to neither Natalie nor John Paul.

Talking over the whispers, Guy Barnes continued, "And as film producers, it is imperative to find the perfect filming location. It just so happens, people of Berlin, that this town, *your* town, is indeed a perfect location."

"Because of power lines?" asked Mr. Brushmiller again.

"Because of *lack* of power lines," Mr. Barnes clarified.

Mr. West stepped up next to him and took the microphone to speak over the anxious crowd. "I know it seems silly but we spend countless hours and a vast amount of money trying to get rid of power lines from our shots, so it is almost too perfect that you don't have power lines in your downtown." He watched the crowd and waited for any sort of response. When none came, he continued, "So, kind people of Berlin, as Mayor Harrison said, we'd like to borrow your town for a little while to film a movie."

The whole town hall came to an abrupt silence. Natalie looked at John Paul who gave the same puzzled look. *What did a movie have to do with the train station or Frank Price?* she thought to herself.

Mr. Barnes leaned into the microphone and said, "And on that note, we'd like to introduce someone to you."

He motioned to the door and the thin woman from the limousine emerged. People gasped. Then the gasps turned into cheers and whoops as the woman walked as if upon a cloud toward the podium.

Chapter 17

In front of all the residents of the small town of Berlin, Maryland, was Juliette Charles. *The* Juliette Charles. The hottest new actress in Hollywood, starring in four blockbuster movies in the past three years and most recently signing an endorsement deal to be the new face of Chanel.

The Mayor lifted his arms into the air to settle the crowd. The actress, unfazed by the commotion, stood at the podium next to Mr. West and Mr. Barnes. Her eyes, a deep, rich blue, stared out at the crowd, casting a spell over all in attendance. Her mouth formed a thin line across her face and conveyed no signs of joy, but her eyes appeared to smile.

"Ladies and gentlemen," Mayor Harrison bellowed into the microphone causing the speakers to squeak. The fanatics dulled enough for him to continue. "As you can see, these men are completely serious. They'd like to spend the next two weeks using our downtown to film scenes for a movie that is staring..."

he angled his arms to draw even more attention to the woman, "Juliette Charles."

This reignited the chaos. The deafening noise caused a ringing in Natalie's ears. John Paul had been trying to say something to her, but she couldn't make out a word with all the noise. Finally, he grabbed her elbow and yanked her out of the row.

As they neared the entrance door, John Paul stopped suddenly, causing Natalie to run right into him. She peered around him and immediately realized why he had stopped. Standing in the doorway was a figure wearing a long, black trench coat. His face was darkened by the setting sun behind him, but Natalie could tell he was staring at the stage.

Natalie glanced back and saw the actress smiling and whispering something to Mr. Barnes. Mayor Harrison was looking out over the crowd with a smirk across his face, and Mr. West was staring in the direction of the man in the doorway. Confused, Natalie shot a look back, but the figure had already disappeared.

John Paul tugged on Natalie's arm again and the two snuck out of Town Hall.

"So, that's what they are here for! A movie! That's amazing!" John Paul explained as he paced in front of Natalie. "And with Juliette Charles, too! My friends will never believe this!"

Natalie kept trying to get a glimpse around him to find the trench-coat mane, but all she saw was a small, black dog in the distance. *The* small, black dog.

Without taking a moment to think or even respond to John Paul, Natalie sprinted after the dog. As she rounded the corner onto Main Street, she skidded to a stop in the middle of the four-way intersection and watched the trench-coat figure walk up the sidewalk on Jefferson Street toward…

315.

Even in the fading light, she watched as the figure turned around, put his hand to his mouth, and let out a high-pitched whistle. The black dog's ears shot up-right and ran across the lawn, onto the front porch, and into the house.

Then Crazy Ernie walked in and closed the door behind him.

@news_in_gray

Grayson Guilfoyle
Reporter of the stars for The Los Angeles News

Juliette Charles is scheduled to work with Ryan West and Guy Barnes on a film set in Berlin, Maryland. More details coming soon!!!

Chapter 18

By the following morning, the entire town had shifted their outlook from gossiping about the strange men to supporting their cause. Natalie took the same route into town but found a huge banner hanging across Town Hall that read, "Berlin Welcomes Hollywood!" At every shop, the owner was cleaning windows, scrubbing down benches and lampposts, and even removing trash cans from the public's view.

As she walked to the hotel, Natalie had to admit that Berlin looked like the perfect place to film a movie, but she had a hard time dismissing the thought that there still wasn't something strange about Ryan West.

The fence separating Main Street from the hotel was roped off with yellow caution tape, but with no one around paying attention to her, Natalie slipped under, sprinted across the driveway, and jumped the two porch steps into the hotel. She found John Paul behind the reception desk with the landline phone held up to his ear.

"No, ma'am. I'm sorry, but they won't allow spectators... No, I have not heard anything about extras... I have not seen Ms. Charles and I am not allowed to ask for her autograph... Hello? Hello?" John Paul placed the phone back on the receiver. "Guess they hung up."

Natalie broke out into laughter, which John Paul immediately joined in.

Through struggling breaths, he said, "It's really not funny. This has been my entire morning, and I've been here since 7:00!"

Natalie tried to contain her laughter and said, "Sorry! It's just funny seeing you there, answering the phone, and wearing a tie!" Then John Paul stepped out from behind the desk, and Natalie hunched over in even more laughter at his full outfit.

"Yeah, Mrs. Fritz said I have to stay behind the desk and answer the phone because I can't start cleaning until I get 'appropriate attire.'" He used finger quotes and made his voice sound like Mrs. Fritz to highlight the two words. Then he motioned to his forest green shorts, "Because apparently, shorts aren't it."

Natalie laughed even louder. "You look like one of those old-fashioned schoolboys!"

"Yeah, yeah. Laugh it up," he said, stepping back behind the counter. "So, clearly, I have learned nothing other than that the entire Eastern Shore has found out about the movie and wants to either find a way to meet Juliette Charles or find a way to be in the movie. Either way, I'm of no help to anyone. All I learned is that they will be finished filming and gone by next Friday. Did you find out anything from your mom about the dog?"

"No," Natalie said as she plopped down on the chair under the window. After telling John Paul that the black dog was a rescue her mom had found a home for, he had suggested that she ask her about Crazy Ernie. Natalie had every intention to do so, but her mom picked up a double shift at the hospital, and she never even had a chance to see her.

"I mean… There's definitely the possibility that they just want to film a movie," John Paul said, reiterating his words from the night before.

Natalie had had a hard time convincing him after seeing Crazy Ernie out in public that there had to be some connection to those men. She tried reasoning with him again. "You just don't get it! That man never leaves his house! Not even to go to the grocery store!" She jumped up out of the chair and began to pace in front of the desk.

"I know! You've said that but still… look around!" John Paul motioned out the window where a large white van was pulled into the drive and men were unloading filming equipment. "I don't think they were lying about *that*."

Natalie huffed. "I know, but something just feels weird to me. I don't know. Clearly that guy had something to do with Crazy Ernie, visiting his house and then Crazy Ernie showing up at the meeting."

The phone rang again. John Paul answered quickly, "Atlantic Hotel, please hold."

He covered the receiver with his hand and looked at Natalie, "Listen. I will keep a lookout here for anything suspicious, but I don't get off until two today."

Natalie looked at the ground and nodded, feeling like she would be useless for the next few hours.

"Let's meet at your treehouse at 3:00, ok?" John Paul smiled.

"Yeah, sounds good." Natalie forced a smile in return and turned to make her way out of the hotel.

"Atlantic Hotel, thank you for holding," she heard John Paul say as her hand pushed open the front door.

Chapter 19

"Go put these on," John Paul's Aunt Em said, tossing him a pair of khaki pants. Natalie hadn't been gone for more than fifteen minutes and ten more phone calls.

After catching them, John Paul held up the almost white colored pants. They looked like something a private school kid would wear. "Seriously?" he asked.

"Yes, I am amazed you did not pack a pair, so I found these at Goodwill, and they looked like your size." She hung her purse up on the coat hanger behind the desk.

"Aunt Em, it's almost 100 degrees outside and there's no A/C in this place."

"I know. It's just for a few hours. Mrs. Fritz wants us all to look nice for our guests. Once you've changed, I will walk you through your job for today."

John Paul held up the pants again. *If the guys from back home saw this,* he thought to himself.

A few minutes later, he followed his aunt to the third floor.

"Ok, I'm going to put you in charge of these two rooms." She motioned to The Anna Suite and the Eliot Room. "Just keep a lookout."

John Paul squinted his eyes and looked up and down the empty hall. "For what?" he asked.

Aunt Em leaned in close and whispered, "Listen, I should have told you before you agreed to work here, but strange things sometimes happen here. I don't know why. It's always been that way, but listen," she lowered her voice, "We can't let anything *scare away* Juliette Charles."

"*Scare away?*" he questioned.

"Just if something seems out of the ordinary, make it seem like it was really you."

"I'm not following."

Aunt Em took a deep breath, "Strange things happen here, and they are caused by..." her eyes darted up and down the hall again, "Spirits."

John Paul tried not to laugh. He had thought Natalie was kidding when she said that the hotel was haunted. "You want me to cover... for ghosts?"

Aunt Em looked around in all directions and then said, "Don't say that word. It just stirs them up."

"*Them?*" John Paul asked.

His aunt took a deep breath, "Listen, when those guys called Mrs. Fritz and asked to use the hotel for a movie, she was honestly hesitant to say yes. She knew...," Aunt Em glanced around again as if expecting to see someone, "That weird stuff happens, and she didn't want to draw more attention to it. The hotel has already been struggling to stay afloat, but if this movie is a success, it will do wonders for business! And quite honestly, for the entire town. Please…" she squeezed John Paul's hands, "Please, John Paul, I know you are new here and I know things are… complicated at home, but this would really help us."

Questions raced in John Paul's head, but he just shrugged his shoulders and said, "Yeah, sure. Just act like a ghost."

Aunt Em shot him a stare.

"Sorry," he whispered as if he believed some spirits were listening.

"I'll take over the phones and direct the movie crew. Just stay put here. Juliette Charles is in that room." She pointed to the Anna Suite. "She has been messaging the cafe for food and drinks. When her orders are ready, you will deliver them to her. Do you understand?"

John Paul nodded. His heart pounded as emotions swirled inside. He took a moment to think about how he got to this place at this moment. He knew when summer ended, he'd have to face all of his mistakes again, but for right now, he was going to enjoy this summer job as waiter and busboy for Juliette Charles.

Sweat had puddled on the back of his neck and he wiped it off with his hand.

Even if he died of heat exhaustion while doing it.

Chapter 20

After leaving the hotel, Natalie checked the time on the town's clocktower. 9:00 a.m. Six hours to wait and she had no idea what to do with herself. It wasn't any different than the days before John Paul had come to town but now, she just felt like she was missing something.

She decided to head to the library to see if she could find any more books about the railway and begin her research on the one from Ms. Taylor, but as she walked past the Calvin B. Taylor House Museum, her thoughts shifted to that box of newspapers John Paul had mentioned, and her body shifted directions from the library.

Natalie walked up the steps onto the front porch and pushed down on the door handle. It was locked. She glanced back toward the street where the tri-fold sign stood with the words "Museum Open 9-3 Daily (Except Sundays)" written across it.

She tried the knob again to see if it was just stuck, but the door didn't open. She bit the inside of her lip and jumped off the side of the porch. When she rounded the corner of the house, she spotted Ms. Taylor's car in the drive, along with two other vehicles Natalie didn't recognize.

Maybe she forgot to unlock it, thought Natalie so she decided to head to the back door to find Ms. Taylor, but as she passed by an open window, she heard a man's voice say, "I'm just glad they didn't get the right to film at the station. Who knows what they'd do to that place?"

Natalie immediately ducked into the bushes and peered into the room. Three people were sitting around a table with one of those tiered towers filled with mini sandwiches and breakfast pastries. Tiny teacups sat in front of each person. Natalie recognized the two women but was unsure who the man was.

"Not like anyone could even get in if they tried because he is still the only one with the key and won't give it up to anyone," Ms. Taylor said. "I've been trying for years!"

Old Lady Jones patted her on the shoulder. "We know, dear, but without a living relative, the station and the land will all be given to the town, so it's just a waiting game at this point."

Natalie thought back to the day Ryan West was in the station. She could have sworn he used a key to get in.

"So, he still owns all that farmland?" asked the man.

"Sure does. I came across the land deed just the other day when I was going through some donation boxes upstairs. I don't even know if he charges the Webb family rent anymore." She took a sip of her tea.

Natalie then heard a faint knock and Ms. Taylor glanced at her watch. "Dear me! Look at the time! I almost forgot to open the museum!" She stood up and left the room, leaving the man and woman to indulge in the breakfast sweets.

"Katherine sure does know how to make a spread," said Old Lady Jones, shoveling what looked like a lemon square into her mouth.

Natalie eased out of the bushes and walked around the front. From the side of the house, she watched as two visitors stepped inside. She knew from her tour that Ms. Taylor started downstairs and she could talk for thirty minutes or more!

Natalie snuck in the opened door and tiptoed up the steps.

Once in the backroom, she scanned around but wasn't sure what to look for. She opened and closed a few boxes, not finding anything that stood out. She bit the inside of her lip, knowing she didn't have much time.

On the far side of the room, she spotted a desk that was littered with papers. She rushed over and began to scan over them. She took a deep breath in and held it as she realized that all of the documents had something to do with the Price name. Peach deliveries, train orders, even small misdemeanor charges for allowing people to work on Sundays. *Why does Ms. Taylor care about the Price name, too?* Natalie thought.

Then she spotted the land deed. Natalie had never seen such a complicated document to read but being familiar with the layout of the town and fields, she could easily see that more than half of Berlin's land was once owned, or may still be owned, by Frank Price. She stared at the signature of Frank Price that was on every page. She held one sheet closer to her face and examined the sweeping F and P written in dark, black ink that hadn't faded after all the years.

"If you haven't already noticed, there are no closets in the house. That is because people didn't own as much back then." Natalie's heart jumped at the sound of Ms. Taylor's voice. She frantically tried to put the papers back in order and rushed into the room with the large chest. She slipped behind the open door and peered through the slat. She knew there wasn't much to see in the kid's room but if they headed to the parent's room, she would have enough time to make it down the stairs.

Sure enough, the three people turned right into the master bedroom as Ms. Taylor began explaining the style of the bed frame. Natalie took two quick steps past the door to the bedroom and onto the staircase. She took the steps two at a time, trying to ignore the ones that made a creaking sound with her weight. The front door was still wide open, and she slipped out unseen into the sunlight.

Chapter 21

Natalie couldn't wait until 3:00 to tell John Paul about the land deed so she sprinted back down Main Street, but a figure on the sidewalk ahead of her made her fall back on her heels and slow to a walk.

The tall man wore a light gray suit and a soft blue tie. He pulled at the collar of his shirt. Natalie acted as nonchalant as possible as she moved closer to the man named Ryan West.

Where are you going? she thought to herself.

At that exact moment, her question was answered as the man turned and entered Levinski's, a catch-all type of gift shop with just about everything you could think of from birthday cards to jewelry and t-shirts to flip flops. Natalie knew there wouldn't be anything suspicious about a kid entering Levinski's, so she walked right through the front door behind Ryan West.

She slipped to the back corner and pretended to skim through a rack of t-shirts. Through the clothes, she watched as Mr. West leaned over the jewelry case that occupied the center of the shop and pulled a silver object from his chest pocket. He caressed the top of it, but she didn't have a clear view to see what it was. He was about to hold it up into the light when Mr. Levinski came out from the backroom, causing Ryan West to drop his arm back down.

"I'm sorry to keep you waiting, Mr. ..." Mr. Levinski began.

"West. Ryan West."

"Ah, movie man Ryan West," Mr. Levinski said, chewing a toothpick and taking a spot behind the jewelry counter.

"Yes, but I'm actually here on non-movie business."

"Well, what can I do for you?"

Mr. West hesitated to show Mr. Levinski the object but then he slowly lifted his hand off, like a kid showing a friend a frog he had just caught.

"I was wondering if you could tell me anything about this?"

Mr. Levinski's back stiffened up and the toothpick dropped on the counter. After a moment of silence, he said in a hushed tone, "Where did you get this?"

Natalie watched through the hangers as Mr. West looked down at the object in his hands and responded, "From a friend."

Mr. Levinski shook his head and raised his voice. "I don't know how you came across this, young man! I made this many years ago for someone who I thought was a friend. How some big Hollywood hotshot happens into my shop nearly sixty years later holding it in his hand is beyond me!"

"I told you. It was from a friend. I am not sure how they got it, but I just need to know what it means. Can you at least tell me who you made it for?"

Mr. Levinski turned away. "That name is dead to me! I refuse to help you with this!"

"Please, sir. I just need to know... for my... my friend," pleaded Mr. West.

"Finish your business in this town and go on your way!" Mr. Levinski demanded as he walked to the front of the store.

"I can't help you!" he added as he opened the door.

Mr. West took the cue, so he tucked the metal object back into his coat pocket and walked out.

Mr. Levinski stared out the window and watched the man walk away. Then he popped in another toothpick and returned to the back room.

@juliettecharles

Official account of Juliette Charles
May we bring only beauty into the world

Staying in the most charming hotel for the next few weeks as filming on my next project starts tomorrow! I cannot wait to work with @ryanwest and @guybarnes!

Chapter 22

John Paul had been watching the grandfather clock in the hallway, trying hard not to doze off in the midday heat.

The first tray of food and drinks had arrived five hours earlier. John Paul had followed his aunt's direction to deliver it to the Anna Suite, but when he knocked on the door, he received a slip of paper underneath that said, "After three knocks, wait 10 seconds, enter, place food on the table and leave."

He followed the instructions precisely and when he had entered the actress' room, she was nowhere in sight. He placed the tray on the table and was hoping for at least a distant "thank you," but when nothing came after a few seconds, he just decided to leave as directed.

He quickly began to hate his job with the realization that he wasn't going to see the actress or even speak to her. He had found a small library down the hall and convinced himself that reading a book would be better than standing around doing nothing, but there wasn't one that sounded the least bit interesting. All seemed like what you would find on the shelves of a retirement home.

After two trays of food and an extra five trays of drinks, John Paul was excited that he had only twenty more minutes left on his shift.

Then he heard laughter.

He looked up and down the halls but saw no one. He knocked on some of the nearby rooms, but no one answered.

The laughter grew louder, and suddenly the door to the Anna Suite flew open! John Paul jumped against the wall, not expecting to see the actress.

But there she stood. In a peach-colored robe and with her hair pulled up on top of her head.

"Please tell that child to stop laughing!" she yelled.

John Paul's mouth froze to an opened O.

"Well? Go do something!" she demanded.

John Paul shook his head, trying to knock some speech into his mouth. "Yes, yes, of course," he said, and he rushed down to the second floor where he swore it must have been coming from.

When he reached the landing, he found it to be deserted. He tiptoed around the railing to the long hallway and listened.

Nothing.

His heartbeat quickened.

"Hello?" he said.

There was no response and no more laughter.

He shook his head and turned to walk back up the stairs when suddenly, a high-pitched scream pierced the air. He covered his ears and sprinted up the steps two at a time to check on the actress. He frantically knocked on the door, "Ms. Charles! Ms. Charles! Are you ok?"

To his amazement, she opened the door. "I am fine! But please stop whoever is screaming!"

"That wasn't you?" John Paul asked.

"No! There is clearly a child somewhere in the hotel! Go find them and tell them to leave!" The actress slammed the door in his face.

John Paul pulled on his sandy blonde hair. The clock read five minutes to 2:00. He could very well just leave and end his shift early, but then another scream pierced the air and Juliette Charles opened the door. "I'm telling you, kid! Do something about that!"

Then the laughter returned, and it sounded like it was on the stairs. "What is that?" Juliette Charles asked as she squeezed John Paul's arm.

He wanted to be brave, but his breath was heavy, and he choked out the words, "I dunno."

There was no one to be seen, but the laughter passed right in front of them. John Paul felt the movie star squeeze his arm tighter, but neither said a word.

Then the laughter turned into muffled words, "Just a hop and then a skip," and the curtains on the window at the end of the hall moved to the side and the sounds stopped.

Chapter 23

"Natalie! Natalie!" shouted John Paul in the distance.

Natalie looked up from her *Eastern Shore Railway* book and saw John Paul sprinting down the tracks. He skidded to a stop at the base of the tree and carefully climbed the broken ladder.

"You won't believe what happened!" Natalie said at the same time as John Paul.

"You were right!" John Paul jumped in first. "The hotel! It's haunted!"

Natalie placed a bookmark at the page she had just found interesting and listened to every detail of John Paul's story. By the time he had finished, her face had turned bleached white.

"The girl on the second floor," Natalie whispered.

"What?" John Paul asked.

"The girl on the second floor," Natalie repeated. "It was one of the stories about Crazy Ernie that I was too afraid to tell you… She died there. No one really knows how but Crazy Ernie was involved. He was just a kid, so nothing came of it but legend has it that he pushed her out of the window!"

John Paul shook his head. "That's crazy! What the heck is wrong with that guy? But that's where I first heard the laughter- on the second floor, but then it came to the third floor."

"Did she want anything?"

"Didn't seem like it. She just kept laughing but then it turned to screaming and then she said something about a hop and a skip, and she was gone."

"Out the window?" Natalie asked, confirming his story.

"Yeah. It was straight-up creepy, and I failed at the task Aunt Em gave to me of not freaking out Juliette Charles. She locked herself up in her room after that!"

Natalie tightened her lips together. "I'm sure it will be fine."

"I hope so. From the way she was talking, I think a lot is riding on this movie and the last thing Mrs. Fritz needs is some ghost scaring away the lead actress."

"What do you mean '*a lot riding on it*'?" Natalie asked.

"My aunt just said something about the hotel being in trouble and close to closing."

Natalie thought about her dad's business. "Makes sense. Half the shops in town have closed up in the past year."

"Yeah, so I guess when those guys called asking to film a movie, it was a no brainer for Mrs. Fritz. She hoped the attention would solve her money problems."

"Wait, they asked to come here?" Natalie asked.

"Well, yeah. That's what they said at the meeting last night, too. Found the town in some historic town database or something," John Paul shrugged.

Natalie bit her lip and shook her head. "Just seems weird… I swear Ryan West is here for more than just filming a movie."

Then she went on to recount the events of her day, from the land deed to Levinski's to another encounter with a snippy Mrs. Fritz when trying to find John Paul early. "So, when she said I couldn't come talk to you, I decided just to come here and read the book Ms. Taylor gave us."

Natalie opened to the page she had just bookmarked and turned it toward John Paul. "Look here. It says that Frank Price Sr. was the one who brought the railroad to Berlin. He owned acres of peach farms and wanted to ship them to New York, Philadelphia, and Baltimore. He built his house right next to the station on Jefferson Street. Pretty much the whole town worked for him. He became crazy rich and some say he shared his wealth with the town, but others say that he was selfish and kept it all within his family. No one really knows the truth."

John Paul finished skimming the section Natalie had shown him and looked up. "Maybe you're right…" he began but stopped short as a beat-up car engine rolled down the street.

He and Natalie peered over the edge to see a red pickup truck pull into the train station's parking lot.

"You've got to be kidding me," murmured Natalie.

"What?" asked John Paul.

"That's Levinski!"

Chapter 24

Natalie and John Paul leaned over the edge of the treehouse and watched as Levinski walked to the front of the station.

"Do you think he's the owner?" whispered John Paul.

"Maybe. That would explain why he was so annoyed with Mr. West. Maybe he knows that they've been trying to use the station for the movie," said Natalie.

A moment later, Levinski walked around the corner of the building. At each window, he peered in and tried to jar it loose. He stepped back to the edge of the platform and put his hands on his hips. Then he walked back to his truck, got in, and drove out toward the highway.

"That was so strange," said Natalie. "Ms. Taylor definitely said whoever owned it has a key."

"Now who the heck is this?!" asked John Paul, pointing to a small white car in the distance with its turn signal flashing.

Sure enough, the car turned into the parking lot and Mayor Harrison and Ms. Taylor stepped out.

"Why is everyone so interested in this place?" asked Natalie.

John Paul shrugged and shook his head.

"Listen, Katherine, I am not sure what you expect to gain from visiting here," said Mayor Harrison.

"I just want to make sure nothing seems out of the ordinary, that's all," she responded as she began to walk around the station. "The thing looks the same as it has for sixty years!"

"And I want to keep it that way!" demanded Ms. Taylor. "We are so close, Mitch. We just have to wait out the old man a little longer and then it is ours."

"Trust me, I know. I already have developers on call when the town finally acquires all his land," added Mayor Harrison.

"And there may still be the chance that..." began Ms. Taylor.

"Katherine, you truly need to stop believing old wives' tales. You know as well as I that there's nothing hidden here."

"But it's still possible! And it will solve all of our problems!"

"Listen, we came here and everything looks fine so let's just head back," said Mayor Harrison. "Plus, this place gives me the creeps."

"And you're telling me that I'm the one who believes old wives' tales?" joked Ms. Taylor as she walked to the passenger side of the car.

"At least my fears are matched by police records!" exclaimed Mayor Harrison, opening his car door.

"Yes, which were never proven!"

Both slammed their car doors shut and after another minute or two, the car peeled out of the gravel lot.

Natalie sat back up and crossed her legs. She placed her elbows on her knees and rested her chin in her hands. "What the heck is going on?"

"There's definitely more to this story that we don't know," said John Paul, sitting up as well.

"So, what do we do now?" asked Natalie.

"We do everything to find out anything we can. I'll do some investigating at the hotel and you can try to get back into the museum. Maybe offer to help Ms. Taylor and see if you can find any other clues. She did say she needed volunteers to go through all the donations."

"I can do that," said Natalie. "I'll look more into that land deed and see what else I can find." She stared out across the cornfield.

"Can I ask you something?" said John Paul.

"Sure," said Natalie.

"Are you still working on building this treehouse?"

Natalie did not expect that to be his question. She knew she didn't want to tell him the truth, so she simply said, "It's a work in progress."

Chapter 25

Ryan West sat in his producer's chair witnessing Juliette Charles dazzle in front of the camera. After closing Main Street on Tuesday, the crew had put in three solid days of filming, and he still had to pinch himself every so often to make sure it was real. He knew he only got the position at West Coast Studios because of his mom, but he had worked hard to prove his worth.

But with working twelve to fifteen hours a day filming, he could not investigate what the items left by his mom meant. One of the only clues he had was a dead end.

As the next scene commenced, the kind woman from the hotel named Emily brought him a glass of iced lemonade. He had mentioned that the lemonade reminded him of the kind his grandmother used to make, so Emily had made a point to serve him a glass every day at noon. She didn't speak much but after handing him the lemonade, she stayed to watch the scene.

Ryan's eyes diverted from his job to watch the sunlight reflect in Emily's hair. Her hair was naturally light brown, but when the sun hit the silky locks, it glimmered with a golden hue.

"Cut!" shouted Guy Barnes. Ryan pulled himself from his trance as the director slammed his hand on his knee and hopped out of his chair.

"No! No! We need to do that all over again! This whole movie is an absolute disaster!" He stormed over to consult the leading actress.

"I thought it was terrific," Emily mumbled under her breath.

"Yeah, Guy will spot a fly zoom on screen and call it quits," Ryan responded to her. Emily smiled at him and opened her lips to say something but was distracted by a frantic Ms. Taylor, who had just cut across the movie tape and walked onto the set.

"Mr. Barnes!" she called, waving her hand in the air.

Guy spun away from Juliette Charles to face Ms. Taylor.

"I'm sorry to interrupt you at work, but do you have a minute to talk?" she asked.

Guy snapped, "No! Not now! Can't this wait until later?"

"It's somewhat urgent!" insisted Ms. Taylor.

"Later!" Guy snapped.

Ryan was about to intervene, but Ms. Taylor accepted the rude remark and walked away.

Emily shook her head at the interaction and then looked back at Ryan. "Enjoy your lemonade," she said.

Ryan jumped out of his seat. "I can get you a chair if you'd like to stay."

Emily smiled again. "That's thoughtful. Thank you, but I do have to get some work done inside. Let me know if you need anything else."

She walked away as Guy shouted, "And action!"

Ryan forced himself to return to his work but continued to glance at the hotel every few minutes.

@juliettecharles

Official account of Juliette Charles
May we bring only beauty into the world

Had an amazing few days of filming! Heading out this evening to throw the opening pitch for the local little league summer season. Be sure to check out my live story at 5 pm EST!

Chapter 26

Three days had gone by without a single drop of rain to ease the summer heat, nor any drop of clues to help Natalie and John Paul solve the mystery they had stumbled upon.

The entire Main Street from Cedar Avenue to Burley Street had been roped off, which meant that Ms. Taylor decided to close the museum for a few days since there wouldn't be any car or foot traffic, meaning that Natalie was unable to follow through on her plan. Meanwhile, John Paul had been swamped attending to Ms. Charles' every need and keeping a lookout for any more ghosts.

Finally, by Friday, he had a moment free during the day and met Natalie on the bench outside the hotel. The movie crew was in between shots, so he was able to sneak her in.

"Fancy badge," Natalie said, looking at John Paul's "CREW" name tag.

"Yeah, Mrs. Fritz asked for the hotel staff to have them since we are the ones taking care of everyone. Most of the rooms are now filled with all of the movie crew!"

"So, have you heard anything suspicious?" Natalie asked.

"Nope. Nothing. From any ghosts or from Ryan West. You?"

"Same. With the museum closed, I really didn't know where else to go. I've spent a few hours staking out at Crazy Ernie's- but nothing… I haven't even seen the dog around!"

"Dang. On the plus side, I heard the whole town is gathering at the baseball game tonight. Juliette Charles is throwing the opening pitch! Aunt Em said it's a tribute game to a player who died. She said to ask you about it."

Natalie's heart stopped. "Um… Oh, yeah. I heard that was happening."

John Paul nodded as if that was the only answer his Aunt had expected him to receive. "So, will you be there?" he asked.

Natalie stood by the concession stand at 5 pm as promised, biting the side of her nail and wondering how to tell John Paul the truth. She liked that he was new to town and didn't look at her like most townspeople do. That sad, pathetic, "I feel bad for you" look, but with Juliette Charles throwing the opening pitch, there was no way she could avoid the baseball game as she had initially planned.

John Paul popped out from the other side of the concession stand and shouted, "Want anything before we go in?"

"No, thank you," said Natalie, switching to another nail to chew on.

While she stood there waiting, Guy Barnes and Ms. Taylor walked past her. "All the records indicate such. There's no other explanation where it all went, and it definitely explains his attachment to the place," said Ms. Taylor within earshot of Natalie.

Natalie wanted to follow them and find out what they were talking about, but John Paul still had two people in front of him and what she needed to tell him was much more important.

A few moments later, John Paul walked up with two armfuls of food. Natalie dropped her hand from her mouth and cleared her throat to speak the truth but the announcer began from inside the ballpark, "Ladies and gentlemen!"

John Paul's face lit up. "It's starting!" He gently nudged Natalie's arm to have her follow along into the stands. As he emerged from the tunnel, he exclaimed, "What an incredible field!"

As they walked up the shiny new silver bleachers, Natalie panicked and said to John Paul, "Listen, there's something I didn't tell you because I wasn't sure how…" but the announcer cut her off again.

"Welcome to the memorial game for Matthew Carpenter!"

Natalie's face dropped. The announcer continued, "We'd like to invite the Carpenter family out to accept this plaque for one of our town's most beloved young athletes and the reason that we are all able to enjoy this beautiful ballpark." Tears swelled in Natalie's eyes.

John Paul turned to face her, hot dogs and nachos nearly falling out of his arms, but before either could say anything, she felt an arm wrap around her shoulder and was led down the bleachers and onto the field.

"I'm glad you came," said her older sister as they walked toward home plate. They were met there by their mom and dad. The announcer continued to speak but it was muffled inside Natalie's ears. The bright lights blinded her, and she couldn't tell if John Paul had hung around or not.

Her family began to receive hugs from a long line of people. Then her brother's head baseball coach handed her dad a plaque with Matthew's name on it that read "#1 on the field, #1 in our hearts."

Natalie couldn't escape. All she wanted was to run far away.

Her mind pounded. She suddenly felt a stab of guilt deep in her stomach, regretting that she hadn't told John Paul. Then she felt even more guilty because she didn't want to be a part of her family any more, especially now as their whole town honored her brother in a stadium that he never even got to play in.

He should be here, Natalie thought.

She wiped her nose with her hand and felt her sister squeeze her tighter. Juliette Charles had joined the row of people giving their sympathies. When the famous actress approached Natalie, she bent down in front of her and said something, but all Natalie could hear was the pounding in her ears. Then the actress hugged her. She smelled like springtime after a morning rain. For a second, Natalie's whole world stopped. When the actress pulled away, Natalie could finally hear the crowd cheering for her brother, and somewhere deep inside of her, she knew that he could hear it, too.

Chapter 27

"Natalie!" John Paul shouted as he waved her over to the first-row bench. She was still numb from all the attention, but when she saw that John Paul hadn't run away, a warm sensation rushed through her body like a sudden cascading waterfall.

As she approached him, she noticed that he was sitting next to Ms. Taylor and a man Natalie recognized from the museum the other day. He was plump and had a poofy white beard and a shiny bald head.

John Paul stood up when Natalie reached him and said, "Ms. Taylor wants to introduce you to Mr. Pullman. He is the museum curator of the train station in Snow Hill. The place she was telling us about."

The man with the bald head rose from his seat and reached out his hand. When Natalie accepted the shake, his sausage-sized fingers wrapped around her hand and squeezed tightly.

"It's so wonderful to meet a young ferroequinologist," he said with a smile as white as his beard as he vigorously shook Natalie's hand up and down.

"A ferroequinologist?" Natalie asked, jumbling the pronunciation.

"A train enthusiast. A lover of trains. A believer in tracks."

Natalie nodded, "Oh, yes. Ms. Taylor must have told you. Honestly, it's just a recent interest."

"All the better! I love meeting a newbie. Ms. Taylor said you were looking up some history about the old train station here."

"Yeah, I'm having a hard time, though."

"Unfortunately, that's the way it is with most of the stations on the shore. It took me seven years to acquire Queponco and turn it into a museum, and I'm still working on gathering up items and information. I've been trying to help Ms. Taylor convince your Town Board that we should do the same for the Berlin station. The train stations may not get a lot of tourists, but they are part of our history and worth preserving."

"You want to turn our train station into a museum?" Natalie asked.

"Absolutely! With Ms. Taylor's help, of course. I feel like if we at least secure all the old stations on the shore, there may even be the hope of starting up the trains again."

It was hard for Natalie to contain her smile. Even as a new *ferroequinologist*, she always thought train travel was something magical, and she smiled, thinking about all her brother's made-up stories as they were first building the treehouse.

John Paul jumped in, "Is there any way we could swing by your station and learn a little more?"

"I'd love that! If you two are free tomorrow, I can meet you there around 11:00 and show you around."

"That'd be great! Thank you!" said John Paul.

"Of course! I look forward to seeing you both! I should be going. I don't want to be seen fraternizing with the enemy." He winked and shook both their hands before heading to the opposite bleachers behind the Snow Hill team.

John Paul led the way up to the top row to take a seat and began to watch the game intently. Natalie was grateful he didn't ask questions. They watched a few innings in silence, and then Natalie asked, "How do you plan on getting down to Snow Hill?"

"It's just south of here, right? Can't we just walk?" asked John Paul.

"It's about twenty minutes by car. I'm not sure how long the walk is."

"Why don't we just take the train tracks? It's probably a more direct route," John Paul suggested.

"I bet it's still a good six miles."

"Then we will leave early," John Paul said, watching as a player from Berlin hit the ball into the outfield leading to a two-run gain that would help seal the team's victory with an 11-4 lead at the bottom of the 8th.

"Woohoo!" he shouted, and Natalie joined in the celebration of cheers and claps.

Chapter 28

Natalie stepped into the morning sun, took a deep breath, and soaked up the brisk air. There was a slight dew on the grass, reminding her that even amid summer, you never knew what kind of weather to expect from the Mid-Atlantic.

She took the route to her old elementary school, where she had planned to meet John Paul. As she turned into the school's main entrance, she spotted him standing on top of the large statue of Burleigh the Bear in the center lawn.

"Ready for an adventure?" he said with a grin, holding his hands to his hips like an overgrown Peter Pan. He jumped off the edge of the statue and landed with a thump on the high grass since he didn't have any fairy dust to make him fly.

"Sure am!" Natalie said, holding up her backpack filled with the essentials of water, beef jerky, and Martin's Old Bay potato chips.

"Lead the way," John Paul said, escorting Natalie with open arms.

As they walked around the side of the school, Natalie's mind filled with old memories. Unexpectedly, she said to John Paul, "You know what the worst part is about growing up in a small town? No matter what you do, your teachers and your parents always find out! I swear they have each other's numbers on speed dial. If you threw a paper airplane across the room in math class, your mom and dad knew before you could even make up a story that it wasn't you."

"Did that happen to you?" John Paul asked.

Natalie chuckled to herself, "No, that time was Matt." It felt oddly satisfying finally saying his name out loud to John Paul. She then added with a smile, "I did convince my whole class to throw their math books out the window before class, though."

"Was there something you guys had against math teachers?" John Paul laughed.

Natalie laughed with him. "I guess I never really thought of that. They were just easy targets. One time, we let all the frogs out of the science lab straight into Mrs. Humphries' math class. Took us the whole afternoon to gather them back up!"

John Paul laughed as he approached the small chain-link fence that separated the playground from the train tracks. "Here, give me your foot," he said as he bent down on one knee and placed his hands into a cup.

Natalie tossed her backpack over the fence and then placed her hands on his shoulders and her right foot in his palms. John Paul said, "1, 2,... 3!"

He pushed up just as Natalie jumped and she cleared the fence by a good foot. John Paul tossed his own backpack over and then took a few steps back for a running leap. He soared clear over the fence and landed next to Natalie.

She tossed his backpack at him and said, "Don't worry. I have plenty of hilarious stories about the troubles Matt and I used to get in to pass the time."

"Well, I definitely learned not to bring up anything to do with math and to avoid frogs when I'm with you!"

They both laughed and began their walk.

When the morning dew had finally evaporated off the grass stems and flower petals, John Paul and Natalie had already covered all sorts of topics; school, sports, friends, family.

Natalie found it therapeutic to talk about her brother finally. Her whole life was filled with memories of him, and ever since he'd passed, time had fallen into a dormant state, like a puddle of water that never moved and only gathered mosquitos and algae.

Natalie and Matt had been inseparable. Ever since preschool when a girl named Meredith Wright poured apple juice on Natalie's head for playing soccer with the boys, she had learned that it was just easier to hang out with Matt. It only started getting weird when girls in her class began to have crushes on boys the year above - Matt included. Then came the girls wanting to be friends with her simply to get an invite to her house so they could see Matt and his friends.

But then he got sick.

And then people found it tough to be around a sick kid, so it was back to just Nat and Matt. Part of her loved that last year the best.

When Natalie realized she had been talking for an hour straight, she gave John Paul the floor.

He shared that it was just he and his mom growing up, and his friends weren't the best influence. He spent most of his time doing dumb stuff with them, like lighting things on fire or skating where they weren't supposed to. He said his mom was going back to school to be an x-ray technician.

He barely mentioned his dad except to say that he had recently found a picture of him and his mom in a box at his aunt's house.

They walked in silence for a little while after that. Natalie couldn't imagine not having her dad. Even when he lost his job and the bills piled up from Matt's treatments, he was out walking dogs and mowing lawns like a twelve-year-old just to try and make some extra money. She appreciated him a little more after listening to John Paul.

With just empty fields lining the tracks and the sun inching higher in the sky, Natalie's heart rate picked up and a bead of sweat materialized on her forehead. "What happens if we go all this way for nothing?" she asked.

"Then we can just chalk it up to an adventure," John Paul said, slapping Natalie's back. "But that guy seems to know a lot about the train history around here, so we are definitely going to learn something new."

"I just hope it's something that is useful," said Natalie, begrudgingly.

A loud shotgun blow sent John Paul quivering to his knees with his hands over his head. Natalie walked over and patted his back. "Just some shore folk, probably." Natalie glanced around to try and find the source. The fields were covered with duck blinds, so it could have been from anywhere. "We should pick up our pace."

Chapter 29

When they had reached the crossroads at Patey Woods Road, John Paul glanced at his phone. "We still have 30 minutes until he arrives. Should we grab an early lunch?" He nodded toward the small diner that sat opposite the train station.

"Sure," said Natalie.

They asked to be seated by the window to watch for Mr. Pullman. After ordering, Natalie stared at the train station and was amazed at its similarity to the one in Berlin. A small rectangular base, a slightly sloping triangular pyramid as its roof, and windows lining all sides. The sign hanging off the gutter read "Queponco."

They ate mostly in silence as anticipation of their meeting heightened. John Paul slurped the last of his soda and nodded at the window, "I think that's him."

A car had just pulled into the gravel drive in front of the station and a familiar rounded head bobbed out of the driver's seat.

"Let's go!" Natalie said as she reached into the front pocket of her backpack and left a twenty on the table. They both stood up and pushed their chairs in.

"Thanks for popping in!" shouted the waitress who was taking an order at another table.

"Thank you," John Paul and Natalie said in unison.

Mr. Pullman was still fumbling with keys when they walked past his car and onto the wrap-around platform. He nodded his head briefly in their direction and his eyeglasses dropped lower on his nose.

"Need some help?" asked John Paul.

Mr. Pullman wiggled the keys in the air. "Just one more to try!" And the lock clicked open.

"In, in! I'll get the fans running," Mr. Pullman said as he ushered them into the station.

Once inside, Natalie could see the similarities between this station and the one in Berlin, but hand printed descriptions were laid next to every item on every old steel and wooden table and chair. The pictures were polished and labeled with tiny white stickers indicating the place, time, and names of the people or objects in them.

Natalie's mind raced across history. She ran her hand gently over the old wooden desk pressed up against the wall. She stared into the faces of all the people hanging on the walls. They all looked so happy.

"This is pretty incredible," Natalie said.

"It's just a slight passion of mine," said Mr. Pullman. "My granddaddy was a conductor for the Eastern Shore Railway. Told me all sorts of stories as a young boy and I just never could let go of it, even long after he had died and the trains stopped running."

He set his briefcase on a table near the window. "Let me give you the tour."

Though the station was far smaller than Berlin's, it was set up very similarly, with the main ticket area and then two offices on either side. The tour lasted about five minutes and Natalie learned that the one office was the depot chief's sleeping quarters. It was set up with a small twin bed and nightstand. There was a trunk tucked under the window that was left open to reveal age-appropriate attire.

Mr. Pullman continued with his history lesson. "This station was more of a cargo load for the Price peaches. Few passengers departed from here. This area was for the Price workers to come to give their daily totals." He waved his hand through the room that Natalie had thought was the ticket office. He walked over to a tall pulpit-like structure and opened a book that rested on top. It looked almost identical to the one in Berlin. "They recorded everything in this train log." He skimmed through the pages. "All the way up to 1960."

"What happened then?" asked Natalie.

"Well... This station had to close because the peach blight hit and these farm stations running along the Price land had nothing left to send so the trains stopped coming. Then eventually, once the second Bay Bridge was built and the highway stretched past all the small towns, there was no reason to keep them open."

John Paul cleared his throat, "You said the Price land."

"Oh, yes. The Price family owned all the land in Berlin and surrounding towns for twenty square miles. One of the first families to truly settle in this region and did it right. Made a fortune! True businessman, that Frank Price. Had some tricky ways of securing more land, but it worked." Mr. Pullman walked over to a shelf filled with large, leather-bound books and pulled one down. He flipped through the pages and then turned it toward Natalie and John Paul, pointing to a photograph.

Natalie's mouth dropped open. The black and white photograph showed a family of four; a man, his wife, a son about nine or ten years old, and a little girl no older than five. They stood in front of a house that Natalie was able to recognize, even without all the years of neglect.

"That there," said Mr. Pullman, pointing to the man in the photograph. "That's Frank Price, Jr. It was his dad who brought the railroads here and started the peach farms. Every peach consumed on the east coast at that time came from the Price orchards. Once he passed, his son took over."

"Is this the same Frank Price with the station fire in Berlin?" Natalie asked.

Mr. Pullman lowered his eyes and nodded. "Yes, that was a shame. The first station in the area and gone just like that. I know what the stories say about that fire but Frank Price, Jr. didn't die that night, but I know that the pain from it eventually led to his death. Well, not totally. But definitely the icing on the cake after what happened to his daughter and then his wife." Mr. Pullman stared at the photo. "They all looked so happy here, too."

"What happened to the son?" Natalie asked, pointing to the young boy in the photograph.

"He grew up and decided to take over the family business. Even lost the love of his life over it. But he never could make his daddy proud after what had happened to his sister." Mr. Pullman took a step back, shaking his head. "All we can do now is preserve the history of the trains."

Natalie wanted to ask more questions, but it seemed that Mr. Pullman was done sharing any more details so she just asked, "May I see that photograph?"

"Of course, of course. Look at anything you wish. I have some documents to file in the office. Look around and let me know if I can help with anything."

When Mr. Pullman was out of sight, Natalie carefully peeled off the plastic sleeve covering the photo and slid it out of the book. "You know whose house that is, right?"

"Yeah, and it looked a lot nicer back then! But what does Frank Price have to do with Crazy Ernie?" asked John Paul.

Natalie flipped the photograph over. On the back were four names and a date. *Frank Price Jr., Edith Price, Frank E. Price III, Addison Price, 1948.*

Natalie almost dropped the picture.

"What?" asked John Paul.

"I can't believe it," she said as her eyes narrowed in even more on one name. "I knew something seemed different about that land deed I saw at the museum. It was the signature! It just said Frank Price, but the signatures at the station said Frank *E.* Price!"

She indicated the *E.* to John Paul and said, "How much do you wanna bet that 'E' stands for Ernie?"

John Paul stared at the names. "So, Crazy Ernie is Frank Price's son?"

"Yes!" said Natalie, trying to keep her excitement contained.

"But what does this have to do with anything? What does this have to do with the station or that Mr. West guy or the movie? It doesn't make any sense," John Paul said.

Natalie's head raced with all the information they knew so far. The train station, Levinski's, Crazy Ernie.

"Mr. Pullman? I have one quick question," she shouted into the next room.

She heard a chair roll back and Mr. Pullman emerged in the doorway. "Of course! Ask away."

"You said that the Price family did it right and made a fortune…"

But before Natalie could get her question out, Mr. Pullman exclaimed, "Yeah, the richest family on the whole Eastern Shore!"

"What happened to all their money?" asked Natalie.

"No one knows for sure. Most say the family lost it, gambled it away or something. But there's a few of us that think Frank's boy just hid it somewhere so no one would ever find it. Money had destroyed everything he loved. His mother, his father, his sister, even his high school sweetheart. Can't blame the old man one bit." Mr. Pullman rubbed his bald head and whispered. "But between you and me...I'd sure like to find some hidden treasure!"

He winked at Natalie and John Paul.

@juliettecharles

Official account of Juliette Charles
May we bring only beauty into the world

You won't believe what just happened! Check out my story for the full details on my encounter with a ghost!!!

Chapter 30

A cell phone rang from the office. "Let me get that real quick," Mr. Pullman said and he rushed into the office.

"That has to be what that West guy is after!" whispered John Paul. "The Price family fortune!"

"Absolutely!" said Natalie. "But how the heck did he ever learn about it? I live here and didn't even know there was hidden treasure somewhere in our town!"

"Maybe he heard it from the friend he mentioned to that Levinski guy?"

"Maybe," Natalie said. "Either way, if it's real, we have to stop him from finding it!"

"But how?" asked John Paul. "We don't even know where to begin to look!"

Just then, Mr. Pullman emerged back from the office. "Anything else I can help you two with? That was the wife. She realized she forgot her wallet in my car, so I am going to run it home to her real quick."

"I think that's all for now," said Natalie. "This was really nice of you, Mr. Pullman."

"Please! Anytime! I'm sorry I have to rush out like this."

"No worries. We should be heading back anyway."

┉┉

After Mr. Pullman pulled out of the station, Natalie glanced up at the dark clouds off to the west. As they crossed the street back to the train tracks, she pulled out her phone to check the forecast but instinctively opened her Instagram account after unlocking it. She ignored the seven likes for a picture of a flower she took the other day and immediately clicked on Juliette Charles' story.

"I think I just figured out the answer to your question." Natalie showed the phone to John Paul and had him replay the video messages and pictures of Juliette Charles' recent encounter with a ghost at the hotel.

"Geeze! Mrs. Fritz is not going to be happy about this," John Paul said, handing the phone back to Natalie.

"Don't you get it? *This* is what we have to do," Natalie said, waving the phone in the air. "We have to scare Juliette Charles out of town. If she leaves, then he'll leave."

John Paul glanced over at her. "That doesn't sound like the best plan."

"Why not?!" Natalie insisted. "Trust me! I've scared away three different math teachers in one year. We absolutely can do it!"

"I get that, but I actually think this movie will help your

town," said John Paul. "Even more than just the hotel. Apparently, the entire town has gone bankrupt!"

"But you said Ryan West had asked to come film here?" Natalie said.

"Yeah, and the Mayor saw it as the perfect way to save the town!"

Natalie shook her head. "But the whole movie thing doesn't even matter! Don't you see that Ryan West has clearly come here for more than just a movie," Natalie pressed on.

"Yes, I agree with you but what if filming the movie really will help save the town?"

Natalie considered this for a moment and then said, "Well, if Ms. Taylor is right, when Crazy Ernie dies without a living heir, the town will get all of his land, which probably includes the hidden treasure!"

"Only problem with that is we have no idea where it is!"

"But Ryan West probably does and is just waiting for the chance to get it!" Natalie shouted.

A crack of lightning lit up the sky to the west. Dark, ominous clouds had swirled closer since they had left the station. Natalie had completely forgotten to check the weather and they were already out of Snow Hill and into the wide-open fields.

Thunder shuddered down from directly above.

"We have to move fast," John Paul said, putting an end to the conversation.

The two broke into a sprint and reached the school's covered entry just as the skies released the floodgates. Natalie flopped down on a bench and opened her backpack for some water. John Paul leaned against a pole and stuck his hand out into the rain.

"I'm sorry I snapped at you back there," Natalie said.

"It's fine. I get it. This is your town."

Natalie chuckled, "Funny thing is though that ever since Matt passed away, it's the last place I want to be."

John Paul made circles with his foot on the ground. "I'm sorry about that."

"I'm sorry I didn't tell you."

"Must have been a pretty amazing person if he was able to get that stadium built."

"It was his Make-A-Wish. He knew he'd never even get a chance to play in it but he still wanted it built for his team."

"Wow. Definitely seems like a pretty amazing guy."

"Yeah, he was amazing," Natalie smiled. "But I did try and convince him a treehouse would be better, but…"

"But what?" John Paul asked, taking a seat next to Natalie.

Natalie picked at her nails in her lap. "But he told me I needed to finish it. He even left all the wood neatly stacked in our back shed and the silly little design we had drawn up together taped to my wall next to my bed." Warm tears began to puddle at the corner of her eyes. She tried not to blink.

John Paul instinctively put his arm around her shoulder and said, "I can help if you want."

The act of sympathy drove the tears straight out of their holders and down the sides of Natalie's face.

Chapter 31

By the time the afternoon thunderstorm stopped, Natalie had dried her tears, made plans to start working on the treehouse again, and finally convinced John Paul that the only way to save the town was to stop Ryan West from finding the treasure first, which ultimately meant sabotaging his movie set. The upside of ruining the town's chances of becoming famous from the Hollywood spotlight was the possibility of finding the Price family fortune, which would hopefully be more than enough to bring the town out of bankruptcy.

On Sunday morning, Natalie met John Paul outside Uncle Ned's Hardware Store. "You sure you know what you're doing?" he asked Natalie.

"Yes, you?"

John Paul looked at the hotel across the street and shrugged his shoulders. "I guess so."

"Trust me. This will work." She patted his shoulder and walked into the store.

As she walked up and down the endless aisles filled with everything from canned goods to garden gnomes, Natalie began rehearsing her opening statements. The pet supplies were in the far back, and their selection of colors and sizes were slim. Natalie chose a bright blue collar and estimated that a medium would fit. Then she picked out a matching leash and found dog tags hanging up and snatched a bone shaped one.

At the checkout, the cashier whose name tag said Benjamin held up the dog tag and asked, "Would you like me to engrave this?"

"Um…" Natalie said. It would make sense to do so, but she didn't know the dog's name. "Just write *Jefferson*."

"No number or address?"

"No, just Jefferson."

When she left the hardware store, she retraced her steps from the first day she had seen the dog. Her plan would only work if she found it and somehow successfully captured it. She searched around the tire piles at Wainwright's, but nothing. Then, she made her way around the back of the hotel, and still no dog.

She finally decided to take a seat on the curb under an old oak tree that sat squarely in the middle between Crazy Ernie's house and the hotel. She pulled out the bag of beef jerky and held it open in her hands. After about ten minutes of waiting, Natalie saw the dog pop its head out of the bushes from across the street. She resisted the urge to run at it. Instead, she pulled out a piece of jerky and whispered, "Here, doggy."

The dog wiggled its nose in the air and began to walk across the street. Natalie stayed seated and waited until the dog reached her hand. She allowed him to slurp the beef jerky right out of it. Then she pulled out another piece. By the third piece, she mustered the courage to run her hand along the top of the dog's head. He didn't run. She laid two pieces of jerky on the ground at her feet and when the dog bent down to get it, she slipped the collar around its neck and clicked it closed.

She let the dog finish his treats and then she stood up with the leash in her hand. "Good boy," she said and patted its head. The dog nudged her side, requesting more jerky. Natalie slipped another piece out of her pocket and used it to lead the dog down the sidewalk.

As she approached the decrepit house, she thought back to the photograph of the smiling family in front of a well-maintained home. She wished she had asked Mr. Pullman more about Ernie's mom, sister, and high school sweetheart, but she felt bad prying into someone's old heartaches. She knew that much. Plus, it wasn't the past that mattered anymore. She needed to find that treasure before Ryan West did.

Natalie took a deep breath and mustered up the courage to walk toward the front door. The dog kept with her. He didn't pull at the leash, nor did he make any kind of sound. Natalie took the two steps to the front door in one large stride, opened the screen, and knocked on the wooden door behind it.

When there was no response, she knocked again. This time, she heard the screeching of a chair against hardwood.

"Who's there?" shouted a raspy voice.

"My name is Nat... Natalie Carpenter, sir."

The wooden door opened, and an old man squinted into the light. "Who?" he asked again.

"Natalie Carpenter, sir. I have your dog. May I come in?"

Natalie had prepared for a fight. She had thought of twenty different ways to approach this man and figured just asking to come in was the best option.

Crazy Ernie glared at her with beady eyes. "Umph," he scoffed but stepped away, leaving the door wide open.

Natalie patted the dog's head and walked in.

The room was dark. All the curtains were drawn tight, except the one facing out to the front. The whole house had a unique stench of mildew and old man soap, like burnt cinnamon. It was littered with books and newspapers; some piled from the floor to the ceiling in certain spots. There was only one piece of furniture that didn't have anything on it; a rocking chair that faced the front window.

Crazy Ernie stepped around some of the mess and began clearing off space on a bench that Natalie realized paired with a piano. On top of the piano were more stacks of books and papers and some photos in frames.

Natalie clipped the dog off the leash, and he rushed over to a water bowl in the kitchen. She walked over to the bench but didn't take a seat. She stared at the stacks of gossip magazines that littered the top of the piano. She was about to ask about them but then her eye caught a silver object, almost buried beneath a U.S. Weekly. Something about it was familiar. She reached down and grasped the metal oval. "What is this?" she asked, more to herself than anyone else.

Crazy Ernie was about to return to his seat but glanced up. Even in a darkened room, Natalie caught his eyes doing a double-take. He shook his head and returned to sitting down without answering her question. Jefferson had finished drinking and took a seat next to him.

"What is it you want? Your mom asked you to come by?"

Natalie glanced up from the silver object. "My mom?" she asked. "Oh, yes! She asked me to get the dog a collar and leash. We have seen him wandering around town and didn't want anyone to think he was a stray."

"I told her from day one that I didn't need a dog!" But even as he said that, Crazy Ernie allowed the dog to lick his wrinkled hand. "And to think, I made the mistake of telling her that it gets lonely around here."

Natalie shook her head, trying to make sense of what he was saying. It seemed as if he had known her mom before the dog. Then she suddenly remembered her mom saying the dog would make a great companion for one of her elderly patients whom she cares for. "I'm sorry. You knew my mom before she brought the dog to you?" she asked.

Crazy Ernie coughed more loudly into the handkerchief. "Course she didn't tell anyone. Helen's my nurse. Been coming here every week for the past five years. Ever since the hospital quit taking my insurance. Joke of a system. Work forty years for the man, give part of your leg in the war, and then when you need some help, they drop you like a box of MRE's in the jungle."

Crazy Ernie coughed again. The dog finished licking his hand and laid at his feet.

Natalie didn't get it. *Why would her mom never tell her this?* But that didn't matter right now. "I came for another reason, too." She bit her lip and fiddled with a small lever on the silver object. "I am helping out Ms. Taylor at the museum and… I… I wanted to see if you had anything you could donate to her new exhibit on the railroad."

"I gave that woman everything I have! What more could she want?" Crazy Ernie shouted into his handkerchief.

Natalie wasn't prepared for that response. "You did and… it's super helpful, but…" Natalie glanced around the room, looking at the black and white photographs in all the frames. Most were of a beautiful woman with long wavy hair. Even in black and white, she looked familiar somehow. A few others were of that same little girl from the photo at Queponco - Ernie's little sister.

"Well, what does she want?" he snapped.

Natalie blurted out, "We are looking for more photographs."

The old man dropped his gaze down to his lap. Natalie could almost feel his pain. He shook his head gently and then nodded toward the piano, "Just tell her she can have it all. No sense in me waiting any longer."

She didn't know what he meant by that. *What was he waiting for?* she thought.

Suddenly, the small silver box Natalie had been playing with popped open and a rhythmic lullaby sprung up and out and clung to the air like the first snowfall. The melody sounded distantly familiar at first. Then, as if the snow turned into a blizzard, all of the puzzle pieces from the investigation began to swirl around her.

"Close that thing now!" shouted Crazy Ernie, rising to his feet and tossing his handkerchief in Natalie's direction. "And get out! Out, out!"

The dog curled up behind his owner as the man shooed Natalie out like a fly that just kept buzzing. "Go! And don't come back!"

Crazy Ernie grabbed the door and slammed it shut on Natalie's heels. She barreled down the front steps, landing on her hands and knees on the sidewalk.

The music box hit the ground and broke into pieces.

Chapter 32

John Paul wasn't keen on the whole plan of sabotaging the movie by scaring away Juliette Charles. He had suggested at least ten other options and noted that if Ryan West wanted the treasure badly enough, he would just find a way to stay in town to find it.

But he found himself in the hotel anyway. It was his day off, so when his aunt appeared at the top of the stairs, she exclaimed, "John Paul! What brings you in today?" She walked down the stairs with a laundry basket full of towels and sheets.

"Natalie had somewhere to be so I thought I'd stop in to see if you needed help with anything," but just as John Paul asked that, he saw Ryan West enter from the conference room.

The man stepped up to his aunt and said, "Here, Emily, let me get that for you."

To John Paul's amazement, Aunt Em handed the basket of dirty linens directly to one of the hotel's guests, and a very important one at that!

"Thank you, Ryan," she said with a smile. "Have you met my nephew, John Paul?"

"Not officially," he said, placing the basket under one arm and holding out his other, "I've seen him around, though. Always helping here and there. It's nice to meet you, son!"

John Paul reluctantly shook his hand. He was never a fan of people calling him son.

It wasn't until after Ryan West turned to take the laundry to the backroom that John Paul realized he never said anything back to him. His Aunt Em was still staring at the man as he walked away. She smiled and then turned to John Paul, "What was it you needed again?"

John Paul squinted at her. She was acting very strangely, but he needed to focus on what he was there for. "I… um… just wanted to see if I left a book here. I'm going to look behind the desk."

"Ok, let me know if I can help," his Aunt Em responded before following behind Ryan West.

John Paul didn't have time to analyze his aunt's behavior. He was grateful to find the reception desk empty and snuck behind it where the spare keys were locked in a case. Each room had three and John Paul had been using the extras for the daily cleaning. He just needed one key now, so he slipped an extra from another room's hook to make it look like it wasn't missing. He dropped the borrowed key into his pocket and then locked the case just as Mrs. Fritz entered from the side door.

"John Paul!" she exclaimed, surprised. "I thought you were off today?"

"I am. But I… I thought I left my book here," he said, pretending to look around. "But I don't see it anywhere."

"What was it called? Maybe I put it in the library, not knowing," said Mrs. Fritz.

"*My Side of the Mountain*," he said. It was the first book that popped in his head.

"I haven't seen that one," Mrs. Fritz said, flipping through the mail.

"I'll keep looking around. Thanks," John Paul said, but he knew Mrs. Fritz wasn't listening anymore. He headed into the lobby and saw Ryan West walking up the stairs. He decided to follow him.

When John Paul reached the top of the landing, he heard someone shout, "When were you going to tell me about this?!"

Chapter 33

Ryan West had not been expecting any visitors to his room.

But Guy Barnes stood in front of the dresser with the contents of Ryan's mother's envelope scattered on top. "I come in here looking for the most recent scene write up and I find all this! When were you planning on telling me about this?!" he shouted.

Ryan hesitated.

"We've been waiting around for some old crackpot to give us permission to film and here you have a key to the place?!"

"It's not what it seems," Ryan pleaded.

"It's exactly what it seems! I know a thing or two about conniving and looking out for number one," he pointed to his chest with his pudgy finger, "But if you want to get ahead in this job, kid, you better not piss off the wrong people!"

"I didn't mean for any of this! I was looking up photos of this town I had never heard of until my mom left me these random things and you just happened to see my computer screen and there was no stopping it!"

"I don't want to hear your excuses! You lied. You lied to Guy Barnes. You better count your pretty stars that anyone will hire you again in Hollywood after I tarnish your worthless name!" He threw the ticket stub and letter back on the dresser. "I'm done here!"

He shoved his way past Ryan West, who was left standing speechless.

Chapter 34

Natalie's hands burned from where they hit the sidewalk. She pushed off with her fingertips and rested back on her legs. Tiny fragments of silver littered the sidewalk. Without moving off her knees, she gathered the ones closest to her and slid them into the front zipper of her backpack. Then she mustered the strength to stand up on two legs and began gathering the rest of the pieces that had been scattered around.

The bottom piece to the music box rolled the farthest away. It skidded to a stop at the gutter of the road. Natalie bent down to pick it up and turned it over in her hands. On the bottom, etched into the silver, was the letter "A." Below that, in print almost too small to read, Natalie made out the name "Levinski."

She stuck this last piece in her bookbag and decided to make a quick stop before meeting John Paul.

The bell to the gift shop chimed as Natalie entered. Mr. Levinski was restocking water bottles in the cooler. His head perked up at the sound. "Good afternoon. What can I do for you today?" He took the toothpick out of his mouth and slipped it into his shirt's chest pocket.

"I was hoping you'd be able to help me with a problem." Natalie unzipped her pouch and began laying out the broken music box on the jewelry counter. "This fell out of my hands today and broke. I'm pretty sure I collected all the pieces, but I have no idea how they go back together."

"Let me take a look." Mr. Levinski pushed up off his knees and made his way behind the counter but stopped a few feet short of where Natalie had laid the pieces.

"Where did you get this?" Mr. Levinski asked.

"I am helping Ms. Taylor at the museum find items for her new exhibit about trains…" Natalie trailed off slightly, not wanting to go too deep into the lie. "This just happened to be something somebody didn't want anymore…"

Mr. Levinski's eyes darted from the silver pieces to Natalie and back. He shook his head and then stepped forward. He grabbed the trash can on his way and Natalie was about to take all the pieces and make a run for it, but then Mr. Levinski stopped. Natalie noticed he was staring at the bottom part where the A was engraved.

"Can you fix it?" she asked again.

Mr. Levinski set the garbage can down and pulled out a plastic container from behind the counter. He began to lay each piece in the box carefully. "I'll see what I can do."

Natalie didn't want to press on any further, but it was urgent. "Do you know how long it will take?"

Mr. Levinski pulled the already chewed toothpick from his shirt pocket and stuck it back in his mouth. "I'll see what I can do," he repeated.

Natalie decided to accept what she could get and zipped up her backpack, just as the bell chimed again. A woman in a bright yellow sundress and oversized hat walked in. Mr. Levinski didn't bother looking up as he said, "I'll be right with you."

He continued to stare at the pieces and assess the damage. Finally, to Natalie's amazement, he said, "I can have it finished by morning."

Natalie wanted to just say thank you and leave, hoping the woman wouldn't recognize her, but as she placed her purse on the counter, she glanced over and said, "Hi, hun. How are you?"

The last person Natalie wanted sympathy from was Juliette Charles.

"Ok," she said.

"Would you like to help me pick out a necklace? I always love getting a piece of jewelry as a memento from every place I film."

Natalie was shocked she didn't mention the baseball game or her brother. She appreciated this and suddenly a rock fell hard in her stomach as she thought about the plan she had convinced John Paul into executing.

"Uh, sure," Natalie said. "What are you looking for?"

Juliette Charles stared into the front case, which was filled with the most expensive jewelry. "Something that says Maryland so when I wear it, it will remind me of here."

"Well, the blue crab is always a symbol for Maryland," Natalie said as she pointed to the little pendant that was speckled blue with sapphire or topaz, or even blue diamonds.

"Yeah?" Juliette Charles said, looking carefully.

"How about something that says just Berlin."

Natalie thought for a second. She never really pictured anything to represent Berlin. The name itself came from some tavern, but then she remembered what Mr. Pullman had said earlier. "There is the peach, I guess."

Mr. Levinski's head turned to face her, but Natalie continued. "There was this family who lived here long ago, and they started a peach orchard. It's what really helped make the town into what it is, or at least, what it used to be," Natalie thought about all the pictures from Queponco of the happy workers and the thriving town. "That and the trains, I guess. The train station was right next to the orchard owner's house!" Natalie realized how stories could be told any way you want to tell them, and in this case, she chose to make it a pleasant one.

"Hm," said Juliette Charles, "Peaches and trains. I like that. Maybe I will find one of each." She smiled her beautiful Hollywood smile and began to look in the case. "Look here, peach earrings! Can I try those on?" she asked Mr. Levinski, who had stopped chewing his toothpick and was still staring at Natalie.

"Yes, of course," he said, turning to the actress. He unlocked the case and pulled out the pair of earrings. They were the perfect peach color and had one orange gemstone that dotted the fruit and one green gem for the stem.

"They are perfect!" Juliette Charles said after putting them in her ears. She turned to Natalie, "What do you think?"

Natalie smiled, "Perfect!"

"Now to find a train…" Juliette Charles said, looking in the front case and then moving to the one closer to Natalie.

"No trains," said Mr. Levinski, "I can tell you that."

Juliette Charles sighed.

"Here's something," Natalie said. "It's not a train but it's a track of some sort." She pointed into the display case at two pendants that touched to make the track even longer.

The actress moved next to Natalie, so their arms were touching. "Well, look at that; it's like a best friend sort of pendant," Juliette Charles said as Mr. Levinski unlocked the case. "I know! I'll take one," she said as he handed her the set, "And you take one."

Natalie stared at the rows of diamonds that made up the ballasts of the tracks. "I can't accept this."

"Yes, you can. If there is one thing I always want to teach young girls, it is that you work hard for what you want, but never be afraid to accept what is given to you."

She found two silver chains hanging on a display rack, ripped the tags, slipped the pendant on, and before Natalie could object again, the actress placed the necklace around her head and cinched it locked behind her neck.

"I don't know what to say," Natalie mumbled as she marveled at the perfect simplicity of the piece.

"You don't have to say anything."

Chapter 35

Natalie had a hard time sleeping that night. Between her bizarre interactions with Crazy Ernie, Mr. Levinski, and Juliette Charles, she had no idea what to think. She rubbed the train tracks pendant between her fingers. She needed to talk to John Paul.

She rolled over to check her phone. 1:17 in the morning. She had tried to call him before bed, but his aunt had taken him to see the ponies at Assateague and he hadn't answered.

Natalie skimmed through their text conversation from the day before. His last message to her read, *There's so much I have to tell you. Let's meet at 8 on the bench.*

She closed out of messages and opened a search browser. She typed in "Price Orchards Berlin, MD." Having a more specific keyword search opened more website hits. She clicked on the first article and began to read.

Price Orchards dominated the U.S. peach market and generated between 250 and 500 jobs in and around Berlin, depending on the season. In today's world, that's a massive employer for an Eastern Shore small town. For over forty years, Frank Price paid out the highest wages than any other man in Worcester County.

Natalie didn't get it. Why were there so many different stories about this Price family? She clicked her screen off and let her eyes readjust to the darkness. She barely knew Crazy Ernie, but something inside her felt that she needed to help him. She had no idea what had happened in his life to make him so bitter, but everyone deserves to be happy.

She would find John Paul first thing in the morning and change their plan… Just a little bit.

The following morning, John Paul was sitting on the bench in front of the hotel at 8 a.m. as planned. When he spotted Natalie, he jumped up and ran across the street. Natalie was about to tell him her new idea, but John Paul cut in first. "You won't believe what happened!"

He glanced up and down the street and then grabbed Natalie's arm and pulled her down the alley behind Town Hall.

He tucked behind a dumpster, pulling Natalie along with him, and nearly shouted, "Guy Barnes quit!"

"What?!" Natalie said.

"Done! Found the key to the train station in Ryan West's room and it pissed him off so much that he just split! Mrs. Fritz told Aunt Em that he left in the middle of the night!"

Natalie didn't know what to think. "But, what does that mean for the movie?" she asked.

John Paul shrugged, tossing his hands in the air. "No director? No movie!"

Natalie was relieved that they didn't have to prank Juliette Charles to stop the movie, but she didn't know what this all meant with trying to find the treasure.

"Is Ryan West still here?"

"Yes, I don't think he even told Juliette yet. I heard him talking to Aunt Em this morning. He wants to wait until after the Fourth of July parade. Doesn't want to upset the town."

Natalie ran her hand through her hair and stared at the ground. The movie didn't even matter anymore. There was so much more at stake.

She shot her head up and asked, "Did you get the spare key?"

"Yeah, but what does it matter? They are leaving and we can find the treasure ourselves."

Natalie went on to tell John Paul about the music box and her encounter at Levinski's. "I need to get into Ryan West's room."

┊┊┊┊

John Paul led the way to the backside of the hotel. "You sure you got this?" he asked, handing her the key.

"Yes, just keep a lookout."

Natalie walked over to the crape myrtle growing alongside the hotel and shimmied her way up the tallest branch to where she was able to reach her leg across to the balcony. She hopped over the railing and walked to the open window of a guest room.

The room was empty, just as John Paul had said. She pushed

her hands in and up on the glass to make it move smoothly. She lifted her right leg over the ledge and rolled the rest of her body in.

There was a large four-poster bed in the middle of the room with an overly large comforter and at least eight pillows. Lace adorned the pillowcases and curtains. The room smelled like a grandmother; mothballs with a hint of lavender.

She took one step and the 125-year-old floorboards creaked. She froze in place and listened to see if anyone had heard. Without any sound in the hallway, she took the last five steps to the door and placed her ear against the wood. She slowly turned the knob and pushed forward. There wasn't a soul in sight.

She sprinted across the hall to the Dickens Room, inserted the key, and slipped inside without another sound. The room looked like the last but had more light coming from the large windows that faced Main Street. Natalie didn't waste any time. She headed to the dresser and pulled the wooden drawer open. Inside, she found a large envelope.

John Paul gave her ten minutes max. She checked her phone. The timer said 90 seconds.

She opened the envelope and dumped the contents on the dresser. She picked up an old ticket stub that said, "Price Station." Every other part was left blank. She set it back down and unfolded a letter. It was wrinkled and the folds looked ready to tear apart after being forced opened and closed so many times. She read the handwriting of the world's most famous actresses.

My Dearest Ryan,

There is so much I wish I would have told you. So much you needed to hear but I never knew when or how to say the words. Now, as I write this, I feel ashamed that I wasn't braver. I don't want to put all of this on you or make you feel like you have to do anything with it, but I just want you to know what I know.

My mother's maiden name was Charlotte Reynolds. She changed it to West when she left her hometown. She never spoke about my father but when she died, she left me this key, ticket stub, and the music box from when I was a little girl. The same music box I played for you every night when you were little. I always believed these items were the clues that would lead me to my father, but I was too afraid to find out. The only connection I found was the name Levinski, which was found on the bottom of the music box. I eventually found a shop of the same name in a small town called Berlin, Maryland. From that, I was able to find the address of the Price Starion off the ticket stub. I sent letters to both addresses, but the train station always came back with a "return to sender, address unknown."

I never received a letter in response from the Levinski address, but I just kept sending mine, hoping that maybe if my father found them, he would write back and want to see me. Wishful thinking.

Again, I don't know why all this matters but I wanted you to know regardless. I love you with all my heart and no matter where the tracks lead, I will be waiting at the end for you.

Love,
Mom

Chapter 36

A girl's laughter from the hallway pulled Natalie from the letter. She had completely forgotten to check the time. There was more commotion coming from outside the door and she heard Juliette Charles scream, "She's back!"

Footsteps sprinted up from downstairs. Natalie quickly replaced the items into the envelope and dropped under the bed. She used her hands to backward slide as far as she could until she hit the wall, but something was digging into her back. She found a way to reach her hand behind and even before looking at it, she knew what she had found.

Just then, the door to the room flew open and feet began shuffling around.

"She's not here!" came the voice of Ryan West as he stepped back out into the hallway. Natalie needed to get out of there. And fast! She gripped the newfound object and slid out on the other side of the bed. She glanced around and saw an open window in the bathroom. She took three long strides and slipped out onto the front porch roof. She tiptoed along, trying to duck beneath the other windows.

As she rounded the corner, she realized that there was no way down. Through the window's curtain, she could see the second-floor hallway, but no one was there. She gripped the object in her right hand and used her left to grab onto the rain spout. She just needed to make it a few feet down and then she could jump but just as she released from the safety of the roof, a figure inside the hotel spotted her and came sprinting down the hallway. In her fear, Natalie lost her grip on the rain spout and fell backward.

She held her breath as she plummeted to the cement below.

But seconds before hitting the ground, Natalie felt two arms snatch her clear out of the air.

Her eyes remained sealed tight as her heart beat out of her chest. She took one deep breath and her senses were flooded with a strong whiff of cinnamon.

Then her whole world went dark.

Chapter 37

"Natalie! Natalie!" came the voice of John Paul. Natalie's world was still dark, but she realized it was because she couldn't bring herself to open her eyes. John Paul placed his hands on her shoulders and shook her body. "Natalie!"

Natalie finally decided to open her eyes and found that she was lying on the sidewalk on Jefferson Street. She couldn't make sense of what had just happened, but as she blinked into the glaring, bright sun, she spotted a silhouette standing in the distance. As John Paul helped her sit up, the figure disappeared into the hazy heat of the day.

"Are you ok?" John Paul asked. "What happened?"

Natalie spotted the silver object lying on the ground next to her and recalled all that had just happened. She replayed the sequence of events to John Paul as he crouched down to listen.

"So, it was you Ryan West saw in the window! He thought it was the ghost, and when he finally figured out how to open it, he didn't see anyone. I searched all the rooms looking for you and then spotted you down here from the balcony. Did you fall?"

"I must have…" Natalie took another look at where the figure had just been standing. "I don't know what happened after that." She knew she would sound crazy suggesting what she thought had actually happened.

"I thought you said you broke this," John Paul said, picking up the object.

"I did. This is another one! Exactly like it! And this one…," Natalie tapped the silver object in John Paul's hand, "I found in Ryan West's room!"

John Paul looked from the object to Natalie. He had found the tiny lever and began to turn it. The lid popped open and the music started to play. John Paul's face validated that he too had heard that melody before.

"We need to see if Mr. Levinski finished fixing the other one, and then we need to find some old yearbooks," Natalie said.

Chapter 38

On the way to the library, Natalie and John Paul popped into Mr. Levinski's shop. He was standing behind the counter, looking over some papers. He didn't even bother to look up.

"Mr. Levinski?" Natalie asked.

The man lifted his head and huffed, "What do you want?"

Natalie accepted his bluntness for just being an old man. "I just wanted to see if the music box was fixed yet. I'm heading to see Ms. Taylor and I'd love to give it back to her."

Mr. Levinski mumbled something under his breath and then scoffed as he pulled out the silver object. "That will be $25."

Natalie looked at John Paul, who looked back at her. He rolled his eyes and reached into his pocket. He pulled out a wad of cash and Natalie gasped!

"They tip well," he said, as he handed Mr. Levinski the bills.

"Thank you," Natalie said to Mr. Levinski, and she and John Paul headed for the door.

"That there's a set. Won't do you no good without the other one," Mr. Levinski said.

Natalie placed her hand on her backpack where the other music box lay hidden. "What do you mean?" she asked, but John Paul elbowed her in the ribs and nodded toward the door.

"Should've kept the other one when I had the chance. Could finally get what's mine," Mr. Levinski mumbled under his breath.

"C'mon," John Paul urged as he pulled Natalie's arm.

Once outside, they found a seat on the bench and Natalie pulled out the music box from Ryan West's room to compare. "An exact match!" she exclaimed as she held the two music boxes next to each other.

"So, what does… ?" began John Paul, but the sudden slamming of a window startled him, and he and Natalie began looking around.

"Let's get out of here," said Natalie. "I think I have an idea, but that's why I need some yearbooks."

The library was empty on the Monday before the fourth of July, but Natalie led the way to the far back where she knew all the town's yearbooks were kept. At the end of every year, her class and all the other grades from kindergarten through twelfth would sign an extra copy of a yearbook that would be stored at the library. Natalie had found this wall a few months ago and was amazed that this tradition had continued back to 1940.

"Ok, that date on the photo at Queponco was 1948 and it looked like Ernie was maybe nine or ten," Natalie said. "So, we are looking for the late '50s to the early '60s."

The two got to work pulling out yearbooks and shuffling through black and white photos, looking for either Frank Ernest Price or Charlotte Reynolds. John Paul was about to pull 1961 off the shelf when Natalie shouted, "I found it!"

He dropped to the ground next to her. "1958. Senior class photos. There is Ernie."

She and John Paul stared into the smiling face of the man now known as Crazy Ernie. "Pretty good-looking guy," John Paul said, which made Natalie laugh out loud.

"What?! I'm not ashamed to say when a guy looks good!" John Paul defended.

Natalie kept laughing as she turned the page to R last names. And there she was. Charlotte Reynolds. Natalie knew the face immediately from the photos at Ernie's house. "He still loves her," she said, more to herself.

"Can't blame him for that," John Paul said, and Natalie instinctively gave him a shove. "What?! I can't say a woman looks good either?"

The two laughed together as they fell into history, finding all the pages that showed the high school sweethearts' love for each other. Sitting on the top of a car in the school parking lot, dancing at prom, even standing outside of the train station that had once stood on Jefferson Street.

Natalie's heart ached for Ernie. "I wonder what happened to them?" she asked. "They seemed so happy. And how does a mother take her daughter and just abandon her father?"

"My mom swears she will never go looking for my dad…" said John Paul.

Natalie felt foolish for not making the connection before she had spoken.

"Would you ever want to find him? Maybe your aunt knows something."

"I don't know. Maybe. But I guess Ernie must have done something terrible to hurt her… That's all I can say about why my mom doesn't ever want to see my dad."

The two sat in silence for some time and then John Paul said, "It's crazy to think that technically all that money will belong to Ryan West if anything happens to Ernie."

Natalie had almost forgotten about the possible family fortune that might be hidden somewhere in town. She went over all the clues in her head again. *The key, the ticket stub, the letter, the music boxes…*

The music boxes.

She leaned forward to grab her backpack and pulled them out of the front zipper. She flipped them both over in her hands to read the bottoms. She was half expecting them both to say "A" to prove they were a match, but that was too easy. The one that she had taken from Ernie's house had an "A" but the other one had a "P" engraved on the bottom. Natalie was amazed at how everything that didn't make sense was now becoming clearer.

"It's impossible," she said to herself.

"What's impossible?" asked John Paul.

"The music boxes... I think I know how to get to the treasure! We need to get back into the train station," she said.

Chapter 39

When Natalie and John Paul made it to the train station, they spotted the black rental SUV parked out front. They both jumped off the tracks and crouched behind a row of bushes.

Ryan West emerged from the driver's seat with his cellphone plastered to his head. "Listen, Guy, you don't know what you're doing! I need what you stole from me back! Please! They're everything to me! And all my mom left me... Please! I know I pissed you off and I'm sorry. But please, I'll do whatever!"

Then he dropped the phone from his ear and took a deep breath. He wiped his face and Natalie recognized that it wasn't from sweat. Ryan West was crying.

He got back into the car and drove away.

When the car was out of view, John Paul said, "Let's go!"

He led the way to the shed on the side and got in the position to give Natalie a lift like he had when they jumped the fence behind the schoolyard.

Natalie placed her foot in his hands and on the count of three, she jumped as he pushed up, and she was able to pull herself up onto the shed. She crawled over to the window and pushed. The window didn't budge. "He must have closed it or something! It's completely shut!" she said to John Paul.

"Just try to push it up," he replied.

"I am!" she said as she pressed on the glass. "It won't move!"

"Pop down. Let's see if there's another way in."

Natalie was able to get down on her own and followed John Paul around the building. He tested every window to see if it would open, but he had no luck. When they made it back around to the shed, Natalie folded her arms and stared out across the cornfield. The pieces were finally coming together.

She looked at John Paul and said, "I just wanted to see if what I remember is right… I mean, it has to be."

"Well, what do you think we do now?" John Paul asked.

Natalie continued to look into the distance and thought about all that had happened in the past week. "It's crazy, but I think I need to give Ryan West the music boxes. He deserves to know the truth."

Chapter 40

The Fourth of July Festival was the most extravagant tradition in Berlin, apart from Fall Fest. The movie set had cleared up along Main Street and most citizens believed it was merely for the festival, but Natalie and John Paul knew better.

All the town's residents strolled the streets where stands were set up with every American food you could think of, hamburgers, hot dogs, BBQ, funnel cakes, and even Maryland's traditional snowball stands. At one end of the street was a stage for the pie baking contest. At the other end was the band stage. Tom Petty's "American Girl" rang through the air, mixed with the sound of children's laughter as they chased bubbles and blew handheld red, white, and blue pinwheels.

"This is amazing!" John Paul said, shoveling his third hot dog into his mouth.

They sat on the bench outside the Atlantic and Natalie watched as Mr. and Mrs. Branson walked by with their poodle,

Mrs. Peters passed out red roses to little girls, and Mr. Brushmiller showed a group of children his juggling skills. She smiled when she saw Ms. Taylor walking the little Abbott boy to his parents after purposely spilling his ice cream on the Yardley girl's lap. *Berlin wasn't all that bad,* thought Natalie.

"Did you spot him yet?" John Paul asked as he moved onto eating his funnel cake.

"No, I haven't seen him anywhere," responded Natalie, craning her neck to look around again. "I'm going to take a quick walk around. Watch my backpack?"

John Paul gave her a salute and she headed off into the crowd of people. She walked to the end of the street where the band had just begun to play a Brad Paisley song and then paced back to the pie contest stand but didn't spot Ryan West or even Juliette Charles anywhere. She was beginning to think that they had already left town with the rest of the movie crew.

She made her way back to the bench where John Paul stood waiting next to her backpack.

"Want to go ride the tilt-a-whirl while we wait?" he asked.

"You just ate all that food and now you want to go spin around in circles?" responded Natalie, raising her eyebrows.

John Paul looked down at his stomach "Good point. Let's go to the game booths instead."

Natalie slipped her backpack on and they maneuvered their way through the crowd to the side of the street where the carnival games were set up. Standing in front of the ring toss booth, Natalie spotted him.

For once, Ryan West was in something other than a suit. He wore bright red shorts and a button-down white collared shirt that had blue stars all over it.

And he was holding the hand of Ms. Hope.

"Is he with your aunt?" Natalie asked John Paul.

John Paul's face scrunched together. "Yeah, don't ask me why or how. Every time she brought him up the past few days, I changed the subject."

"And this isn't something you thought you should have shared with me?" Natalie said, giving him a shove on his arm.

"What's it matter? He'll be leaving in a few days anyway."

Natalie watched the couple weave around the dunking booth, trying not to get wet. Ms. Hope wore a bright blue tulip dress and had her hair in pigtail braids, with little red bows to tie them off. "Well, for what it's worth, they do look cute together," Natalie said, at which John Paul almost choked on his sip of milkshake.

Juliette Charles skipped across the street to join the couple at the pie contest stand. Natalie and John Paul moved closer as Ms. Hope squeezed the arm of Ryan West and said, "You better vote for me."

He squeezed her hand back and said, "If it's as good as your lemonade, then it's guaranteed to win!"

John Paul's face scrunched up again as they approached the happy couple. Juliette Charles had just finished signing a little girl's t-shirt and for a second, there was no one else around so Natalie leaped at the opportunity.

"Mr. West," she said. He turned around and his face went from joyful and smiling to flat and pale white.

"I recognize you," he said. "You were the ghost in the hotel. But..."

"Ghost?" said Juliette Charles. "She's not a ghost. She's the little girl from the baseball game. Don't you remember?"

"I could have sworn it was your face in that window," Ryan West said, staring at Natalie.

"Wasn't me," she lied. "I'm actually here to return something of yours."

Natalie spun her backpack around to her side and unzipped the front pocket. A wave of panic took over as she found it empty. She looked up to John Paul, but her eyes were diverted to see Ernie's dog running and barking madly through the crowd of people. He sprinted straight to Natalie and jumped on her chest as he yelped in her face.

"What is it, Jefferson?" she asked, trying to pet his head.

He kept barking and nudging at her stomach.

"Something's wrong," John Paul said.

"What is it, Jefferson?" she asked again. Then the dog made a beeline through the crowd of people. Natalie forgot all about the music boxes and followed him.

Chapter 41

"Fire!" Natalie shouted at the top of her lungs as she followed the dog down Jefferson Street.

Ernie's house was ablaze in red against the Fourth of July blue sky. With all the neighbors enjoying the celebrations on Main Street, no one was around to notice it.

Natalie dropped her backpack and sprinted across the front lawn. She jumped up the front steps and kicked the door in. A gust of smoke blew out from the house like a fire-breathing dragon. It immediately filled Natalie's lungs and burned like scalding hot water. Her eyes blurred in the haze and she coughed harshly. She moved only from memory as the fire and smoke had already engulfed the entire living room.

When she reached the spot where she knew Ernie's chair sat, she leaned forward and wrapped her arms around the limp body of the old man. With every ounce of strength she had, she pulled him toward her. Natalie stumbled back slightly but regained her balance when a crash resounded near the front door. With one glance, she saw that the door frame had caved in. She coughed again and the smoke filled her lungs once more. With the man's body against hers, she walked backward and dragged him through the kitchen to where Natalie heard Jefferson's barking.

Natalie followed the sound until her back hit a wall, sending pain down her shoulder blades down her spine. The dog kept barking so she knew this must be the back door. She leaned forward ever so slightly to get enough momentum and with one big heave, she threw both of their bodies into the door and they tumbled down the concrete steps and into the grass that had been charred black from the heat.

"Natalie!" came a voice. She felt her body being pulled across the lawn and away from the flaming inferno.

@juliettecharles

Official account of Juliette Charles
May we bring only beauty into the world

MUST share the most heroic rescue story! A 12-year-old girl went into a burning house to rescue an 80-year-old man! Click the link in my bio for more on the story.

Chapter 42

Natalie tried to take a deep breath, but her lungs rejected the motion, sending the air back out in a fit of coughing. "Don't move, honey," came the soothing voice of her mother. She felt her mother's hand press down on hers.

Natalie blinked her eyes open and saw her mother's face. Tears bubbled up from nowhere and her mother leaned in closer and gently hugged her. Her father entered the room and rushed over to her. The three of them crowded on the twin-sized hospital bed as a flood of emotions ripped through Natalie.

Through the blur of tears, she spotted John Paul asleep on a couch opposite her hospital bed.

"He hasn't left," said her dad with a straight face.

Her mother smiled at him and gave him a nudge on the arm. "It's sweet. I was finally able to convince him to get some rest and promised that we would look after you."

Natalie smiled. She knew her parents must be happy she had finally found a friend, but she never dreamed this would be how they met.

Just then, her sister popped into the room with three coffees in her hands. "The heroine's awake!" she said.

"I'm sorry," Natalie struggled to say.

"You *should* be," said her sister. "That was extremely stupid of you." She said this with a smile on her face. "But also, extremely brave. That old man would have died if it weren't for you."

As if the haze of smoke had officially cleared, Natalie remembered everything. "He's ok, then? He's alive?!" She tried to stand, but her dad placed his hand on her shoulder.

"Not yet, missy. You are very lucky you weren't more badly injured, but the doctor needs to get you checked out before you make any sudden movements."

Her mom stepped in and placed her hand on Natalie's thigh. "Yes, Ernest is alive and doing fine. Better than you, honestly."

Natalie was relieved to hear this. There was so much that he and Ryan needed to know. "I need to talk to him… and Ryan West. Can you wake up John Paul?"

"Honey, it's two in the morning. Can't this wait?" But just as her mom said this, a police officer popped into the room.

"I'm sorry to intrude, but I heard Ms. Carpenter was awake and we'd like to get her statement."

"Now?" her mom questioned. "She only just woke up. Can't this wait?"

"Typically, yes, but we suspect this particular incident to be arson, so we'd like to get her statement as soon as possible to continue the investigation."

"Arson?" John Paul said, sitting up on the couch.

The police officer turned toward him, "Yes, based on the initial report from the fire chief, it appears that this fire was man-made. They are still investigating the evidence."

"I'm sorry, officer, but this needs to wait. My daughter needs her rest."

"Mom," Natalie said as she reached for her mom's hand. "It's fine. It shouldn't take long."

After Natalie finished giving every detail of the fire that started with the dog near the pie contest stand to where she was now, the officer thanked her for her time and said he would return if he had any more questions. She was grateful he didn't ask anything specific about Ernie.

With John Paul awake, Natalie's mom patted her hand and said, "We will give you guys some time," and her family headed out of the room.

As soon as they left, Natalie said, "We need to get to the train station now!"

"What are you talking about?" asked John Paul. "You're in no shape to leave!"

"Someone stole those music boxes from my backpack! Someone who clearly knew we had them!"

John Paul pulled his eyebrows together as he asked, "Levinski?"

"Exactly!" exclaimed Natalie. "He seemed super angry when Ryan West brought that first one in and then even angrier when he gave us back the second, clearly thinking there was no way we'd actually have the pair."

"But how would he know you had the pair?"

"I don't know. Maybe followed us or something. But it doesn't matter! It had to have been him! You watched the backpack the whole time I walked away yesterday, right?"

"Yes!" John Paul said, but his eyes shifted to the floor, "Except when I went to throw away the trash." He raised his hand. "I left for maybe thirty seconds."

Natalie was fumbling with the IV's strapped to her arms. "Just enough time for someone to unzip and zip a backpack."

Chapter 43

It was easy enough to sneak out of the hospital as there were only a few nurses on the nightshift. Once outside, a crack of lightning lit up the sky, followed almost immediately by thunder. John Paul grabbed Natalie's arm to slow her down. "Are you sure we should be doing this?"

For the first time in his life, he was the one thinking reasonably when placed in a situation he shouldn't be in.

"Trust me! There's not enough time and no one would believe us anyway!" Natalie insisted.

John Paul shook his head, realizing it would be useless to try and stop her.

The two sprinted along the train tracks but as they neared the station, a golden glow radiated from the windows. "No!" shouted Natalie just as another crack of thunder opened the skies and heavy raindrops began to pelt down on the hot, dry ground, creating a fog of evaporation at her feet.

She covered her head with her backpack and sprinted the rest of the way to the station.

Parked out front was a small black car that had its trunk flung open. Inside were piles of black duffle bags.

Natalie dashed through the open door with John Paul on her heels.

In the corner of the room, she saw an opening in the wall, exactly where the safe was located. She stepped closer, but John Paul pulled at her arm. "Natalie, this isn't safe! We should call the police!"

"No! Levinski will be long gone by the time they arrive!" she snapped at him before tiptoeing closer to the opening where the glowing light shone brighter. As she reached it, she saw a shadow appear at the base of a long stairway. It started moving toward her. She grabbed John Paul's arm and pulled him behind the ticket stand.

She listened for the man to reach the top and as soon as he did, she stood up and shouted, "Stop right there, Levinski!"

The man dropped the bags he was carrying, spun around, and whipped an object out from his belt line.

When his eyes met Natalie's, she exclaimed, "Guy Barnes?!"

"What are you two doing here?!" he shouted, holding a gun directly at Natalie and John Paul.

"We should be asking you that!" Natalie said.

"Ha! You foolish kids. You didn't think I'd hear about this 'secret' treasure and not come looking for it. And no one would suspect me. I'm already long gone and back to California." He stepped closer to Natalie and John Paul, holding the gun in the air. "So, you see, your arrival is quite unfortunate…"

"Why are you doing this? Won't you make more than enough money from the movie?" asked John Paul.

Guy Barnes let out a laugh. "That movie is never going to make it! Should have seen that from the start but then I had a little birdie tell me about a stash of cash hidden in town, and I thought, why the heck not?"

"They'll find you!" Natalie shouted.

"You think a scream is going to save you, little girl? Now, just to figure out what to do with you both?" He glanced around the station.

John Paul pulled at Natalie's arm to get her behind him as they were backed further into a corner.

Suddenly, Guy Barnes let out a laugh. "Oh, it's perfect!" He grabbed John Paul's wrist and pulled him toward him, holding the gun to his head. "Down the steps! Now!" he shouted at Natalie.

Her heart stopped beating and a pounding filled her ears, matching the sound of the rain hammering on the windows. John Paul nodded to her and she moved toward the steps.

"Pick up the pace! Down the steps!"

Natalie took each step slowly with John Paul and Guy Barnes following behind.

When she reached the bottom, she found an empty concrete room. Guy Barnes shoved John Paul into Natalie and held the gun at both of them. "Hand me your cellphones."

They did as they were told.

"Now, turn around and put your hands against the far wall."

John Paul grabbed Natalie's hand as they followed the orders.

"Don't move from that spot!" Guy Barnes said.

Natalie's face pressed up against the cement wall and she stared into John Paul's eyes.

"I'm sorry," she mouthed.

The flashlight that had illuminated the room faded as Guy Barnes disappeared up the stairs.

"Don't move or I'll shoot," shouted Guy Barnes at the top. Natalie whipped her head around to find that he wasn't talking to them.

"Someone else is here," Natalie whispered to John Paul.

"This way!" John Paul said as he grabbed Natalie's arm and pulled her under the staircase.

They huddled underneath and watched through the steps' slats as two shadows from above danced across the floor.

"This doesn't belong to you! It should've been my family's wealth, and I won't let anyone take it away again!" shouted a voice.

The shadows fell out of view and a gunshot echoed throughout the station.

@news_in_gray

Grayson Guilfoyle
Reporter of the stars for The Los Angeles News

Filming in Berlin, Maryland officially stopped due to a dispute between Ryan West and Guy Barnes. More details to follow.

Chapter 44

It felt as if an eternity had passed before either Natalie or John Paul spoke.

"I'm going to go up. You stay here," John Paul said.

"I'm not letting you go alone," insisted Natalie.

"I think they are gone. I'm just going to look."

Natalie nodded and tucked her knees closer to her chin.

She waited as John Paul tiptoed up the stairs. Almost immediately, he shouted down to her, "We need the police!"

▓▓▓▓

The thunderstorm had finally passed, and the sun was about to break the horizon, so John Paul and Natalie both took a seat on the curb to await the arrival of the police. Natalie found a small stick on top of the graveled rocks to stare at and try to forget what she had just seen.

A dead body.

She couldn't even watch as John Paul patted Guy Barnes' pockets looking for one of their cell phones.

Within ten minutes of making the call, she and John Paul were wrapped in blankets and placed on the back of an ambulance. A police officer stood in front of them with a notebook.

"So, let me get this straight. You found two music boxes that you think were the key to buried treasure hidden in the train station, but you say that these music boxes were stolen so you rushed here to find out if someone had gotten to the treasure, which is when you found Guy Barnes stealing it? And then he threatened to kill you but someone else showed up and then you heard the gunshot?" the officer questioned after Natalie and John Paul had told their story.

"Yes!" they said together.

"And that this so-called treasure that you speak of belongs to Ernest Price, who's grandson just happens to be Ryan West."

"Yes!"

The officer wrote something in his notebook.

Another police officer stepped out of the train station, "Um... Officer Hughes, I think you should see this."

Officer Hughes glanced at Natalie and John Paul. "Don't move."

They waited. When the officer returned, he said, "If you are comfortable with it, I'd like you two to follow me into the station."

John Paul held his hand out to Natalie. She reluctantly took it and together, they jumped off the back of the ambulance. They followed Officer Hughes inside, past the body which had been covered by a black tarp, and toward the secret staircase.

But the door was closed, and it now just looked like the wall they had first explored with the safe in it.

Another officer appeared holding two silver oval objects.

"The music boxes!" exclaimed Natalie.

The officer clicked the objects together and placed them inside the safe, right on top of the two letters Natalie had thought were the safe maker's logo. An A and a P. He pushed down and a click came from inside the safe, revealing a hidden lever against the back wall. The officer pulled on the lever and a part of the wall opened like a door, revealing the staircase.

"We didn't believe they would work. The music boxes, I mean," said the younger officer. "So, we closed the door and decided to test them out."

Officer Hughes stood there, dumbfounded. "Well, I'll be..." he said.

"See? We told you the truth! The treasure was here! But we were too late!" Natalie exclaimed. Her thoughts trailed off as she thought about that small stick in the parking lot. "Levinski..." she whispered.

"I'm sorry, miss, who?" asked Officer Hughes.

"Mr. Levinski!" Natalie shouted. "I suspected him all along. He had to be the person who showed up! The toothpick! It was a toothpick outside. And I bet he or Guy Barnes set Ernie's house on fire! As a distraction."

Officer Hughes nodded to the officer who was standing in the doorway to the vault, "Head over to Levinski's. See what you can find."

Then he turned to Natalie and John Paul. "We will look into it, but we don't suspect either of them for the arson…" A commotion from outside led Officer Hughes to stop what he was about to say and walk out front. Natalie and John Paul quickly followed.

In the parking lot, a young police officer was trying to hold back a woman.

"What happened here?!" shouted Ms. Taylor.

"Ms. Taylor," said Officer Hughes.

"I came as soon as I had heard!"

"That's convenient," said Officer Hughes. "Now, you can place your hands behind your back."

"What are you talking about?" asked Ms. Taylor, but her voice began to quiver.

"It was lucky that Natalie made it to the fire when she did. When she saved Mr. Price, she picked up an interesting piece of evidence on the bottom of her shoes."

Ms. Taylor stopped trying to get past the officer and started walking backward to her car.

Officer Hughes continued in closer. "You see. On the bottom of Natalie's shoes, we found a type of chemical. The same type of chemical people used for lanterns in the 1800s."

"So, what does that have to do with me?" asked Ms. Taylor.

"The same kind of chemical you use for demonstrations in your museum."

"That's impossible!" Ms. Taylor exclaimed. "Why would I…?"

"Why would you try to murder Ernest Price?" Natalie finished for her. "Because you were fed up with waiting for his permission to get this building for your next museum, or for the stash of money you knew was hidden here!"

The young officer stopped Ms. Taylor from trying to open her car door, spun her around, and pulled her arms behind her back. She shouted, "Please! I didn't… It wasn't… Guy Barnes promised! It's all their fault!" She nodded her head toward Natalie and John Paul.

"Guy Barnes is dead, Ms. Taylor," Officer Hughes said.

"Our fault?" asked John Paul at the same time.

"Dead? How?" Ms. Taylor asked.

"We are investigating that now and you happen to be one of our prime suspects," Officer Hughes stated.

"This is ridiculous! I was fine just buying my time, waiting for the old man to croak, but then I overheard you kids in the library and somehow, you had figured out that Ernest Price actually has a living relative and you even had the key to his family's treasure! If he or the town learned about that, then all my hard work would have been for nothing! I was doing what was right for Berlin! I was going to give the money to the town!"

"Guy Barnes was stealing it all for himself," said Natalie.

"No! That's not what we had agreed upon! I took the music boxes from you and he took the key to the station. We were supposed to split it!"

"Take her away," nodded Officer Hughes.

His walkie buzzed loudly. Hughes picked up the receiver off his chest and held it to his mouth. "This is Hughes."

"We are at Levinski's and he's nowhere to be seen. Came across some interesting papers though that we thought you should take a look at."

Officer Hughes radioed back. "I'll be right there." Then he turned to face Natalie and John Paul, "And you two are coming with."

Chapter 45

Officer Hughes led the way to his police car and opened the back door. Natalie skipped over and hopped in, but John Paul hesitated. "You coming?" she asked.

John Paul nodded and walked slowly to the car and took a seat next to Natalie.

"This is so cool!" Natalie whispered once the car started heading down Old Route 50. "Is it weird that I've always wanted to ride in a cop car? Not like, as a criminal, but like this."

John Paul gave a slight smile.

The car pulled down Main Street and parked next to the other officer's car outside Levinski's shop.

"Wait here," Officer Hughes said before stepping out.

John Paul began to squirm in his seat and kept glancing around all sides.

"What is wrong with you?" asked Natalie.

John Paul said, "Cops just creep me out a little."

Suddenly, there was a banging on the window and both kids jumped at the sight of Emily Hope. "What did you do, John Paul Waters?" she shouted from outside the window.

Officer Hughes had emerged from the shop with a stack of papers in his hand. "Ms. Hope, is everything ok?"

"What did he do, Officer? My job was to keep him safe and out of trouble here! And now look at him! John Paul, your mother will never forgive me!"

"Ms. Hope, the kids didn't do anything. They are helping me solve some crimes that have recently taken place."

Emily Hope put her hands on her hips and pulled her eyebrows together. "He's helping you?"

"Yes," replied Officer Hughes.

From the look she gave the officer, she didn't believe him one bit. "Fine, let me in. He has some explaining to do."

Officer Hughes didn't object and opened the back passenger door. Ms. Hope slid in next to Natalie, squishing her in the middle. She leaned over and stuck a finger at John Paul, "You better not be in trouble, young man!"

Natalie was confused by what was happening, but she didn't think now was the time to ask about it. Instead, she just squeezed John Paul's hand. He squeezed back.

All the passengers in the back of the police cruiser were completely silent as Officer Hughes drove them to the hospital. When they pulled in the emergency loop, Natalie objected,

"Please, Officer! I can't go back. We need to figure this out! I have to find Ryan West!"

"Calm down. I'm not here to take you back and I already contacted Mr. West and he is meeting us here," Officer Hughes explained.

Ms. Hope turned from Hughes to Natalie, "What does Ryan have to do with this?"

"Everything!" said Natalie and John Paul in unison.

Officer Hughes led the way through the hospital to the third floor. After speaking with the nurses for a brief second, he spotted Ryan West emerge from the elevator.

Ryan glanced around at the people there and said to Hughes, "What is going on here?"

"I'd like to speak in private first," said Officer Hughes and he led Ryan into an empty nurse's room.

Natalie, John Paul, and Ms. Hope sat quietly in the chairs lining the white hallway. Natalie wanted to ask John Paul about Ms. Hope's behavior but couldn't find the chance to get him alone, so she just continued to sit in silence. Finally, the two men came out of the room, and Ms. Hope ran to hug Ryan. He squeezed her tight.

Officer Hughes gave a gentle cough to break up the couple, "These were what I was talking about," said Officer Hughes, handing Ryan a stack of already opened envelopes.

Natalie tried to get a glimpse, but she couldn't make out what they were.

Officer Hughes said, "They are all letters that had been mailed to Levinski's store but each one is addressed, *'To My Father'*."

Ryan West opened one and after reading it, he said, "These are the letters from my mother."

"Seems so. Maybe you can help us understand why," said Officer Hughes, "There's more than a few hundred stored in Levinski's apartment."

"It's unbelievable," Ryan said as he fell into another letter. "Why would he keep them if they didn't belong to him? What was it to him?"

"I think that can only be answered by one person," said Officer Hughes as he nodded to room 16. He then stepped away to the nurse's station and Ryan stared down at the stack of envelopes in his hand.

Natalie stood up from the waiting chair and walked toward Ryan. "These also belong to you," she said as she handed him the music boxes. "Officer Hughes said I could return them."

"Them?" Ryan asked.

"Well, technically, I took one from you. The other one came from Cra-... from Ernest Price's house."

Ryan shook his head. "I thought Guy took mine, along with the key. I was so sure of it. I have no idea how he figured it all out before me."

"I think he had some help with that," said Natalie.

Ryan stared down at the music boxes. "Thank you for these." He looked back up and then over to John Paul. "Thank you both for everything. I was too afraid to find out the truth. I didn't know what good would come from it. I decided I was just going to film the movie and head out, but you both found out the truth for me. For that, I don't know how to thank you."

"But we lost all the treasure," John Paul said, standing to join them. "And that Levinski guy got away!"

"There is more important treasure in life than money," said Ryan West. He smiled at Emily and then opened the door to room 16. "Shall we?"

Chapter 46

"I think you should just go," said Natalie.

"No, I wouldn't be here if it weren't for you both. You need to hear what he has to say as much as I do."

Ryan held out his arm to make sure they both entered before he did. The room was identical to the one Natalie had been in just a few hours before, but lying in the bed was Ernest Price. A hose was strapped to his face, making his breathing sound robotic. He looked like he had aged another ten years since when Natalie had visited his house.

Ryan stepped up to the side of the bed and placed his hand over Ernie's hand. He gave it a light shake and the old man's eyes slowly blinked open.

"I'm sorry to wake you, sir," said Ryan. "But we..." he motioned back toward Natalie and John Paul, "We all were very anxious to talk to you. How are you feeling?"

Ernie stared up at Ryan as if he had known him his whole life. Then he shifted his gaze to Natalie. With a heaving breath, he said, "You the Carpenter girl who saved my life?"

Natalie smiled. "Just repaying a favor for you doing the same for me."

Ernie nodded and then yanked the breathing hose off his face. Ryan was about to object, but Ernie spoke more clearly as he said, "I couldn't lose another life to that second-floor window."

Natalie and John Paul exchanged glances, realizing that he was talking about his sister, the girl who haunts the second floor.

"But I truly don't know how to thank you," continued Ernie. "I had spent so many years wishing my life away and when I woke up inside my burning home, all I wished for was another chance to make things right." Tears began to fill his eyes, making the blue even brighter. Natalie watched as he pulled his hand out from under Ryan's, only to place it on top. Ryan looked down with a confused look on his face.

Ernie looked into his eyes and said, "I should have found you when I heard you were here, but I was too afraid of what I've become and all the mistakes I made in the past."

Ryan took a deep breath.

Ernie continued, "I didn't want to interfere in your life. It was the same reason I didn't seek out your mother. When Charlotte left, I was devastated. It had been our plan all through high school to get out of Berlin and see the world. Then my father said that if I left, I would give up my claim to the Price name - all the land, all the money, everything he and his father had worked to build. At that time, my only thought was the money and once we got married, I thought it'd be enough to convince her to stay but then one night, she just left. I found her name written in the train log, but she had crossed out Price and wrote West. It was a clue to where she was headed. I should have followed…"

Ernie's eyes continued to fill with tears as he reached for his wallet on the bedside table. He pulled out a folded piece of paper. With his frail fingers, he carefully opened it, revealing the last page of the train log. Natalie let out a gasp of astonishment.

"For sixty years, I've kept this with me…" he said as he stared at the last line where Charlotte had written her new name.

"A few months later, I received a letter from her that she had given birth to a baby girl and named her Addison… after my sister." The tears in Ernie's eyes began to flow more freely, and Natalie felt her own nose tingle indicating she wasn't far behind. "I was determined to get them back. I had a friend make me a special set of music boxes that would act as a key when linked together, and then I locked all my family's money in the safe room at the station. I engraved one music box with an *A* for Addison and one with a *P* for Price: her true last name. I mailed the music box with the *P* and a note saying, 'Nothing is worth more than family' to the return address on the leCharlotte's, just praying it would reach her. I never heard anything back. Years went by and I became more bitter and angry with myself. I joined the army in '65. Figured that was the least I could do with the life I had but I couldn't even succeed there. Got half my leg blown off and was sent home with a purple heart. But I had nothing to come home to…"

By now, Ryan and John Paul had pulled up chairs and Natalie found a clear spot at the foot of Ernie's bed.

"Then one day, I walked by the cineplex and saw a name on a movie poster: Addison West. She was only ten or eleven and looked just like her mother. I must have watched that movie one hundred times in a week! She was beautiful and talented and seemed so happy. Charlotte had given our little girl a life of fame and it fit her well. I never wanted to reach out to mess up all she had worked for. I figured if she wanted to find me, she would know where I was, so I just followed her life through the movies and magazines. I even subscribed to five different newspapers in California just to see if there was ever an article about her. Then *The Los Angeles News* arrived one day announcing her death... I died all over again." Tears streamed down his face, and Ryan handed him a tissue.

After wiping some away, he looked at Ryan and said, "And then you showed up here."

Ryan squeezed Ernie's hand and said, "She loved you! She was just too afraid to come find you, but look!" He handed Ernie the music boxes. "My mother played this music box for me every night as a child and always said her mother had done the same for her... And look!"

This time, he handed Ernie the stack of letters. "She wrote to you! She wrote to you every week for the past ten years! There are so many more, too. She wanted to find you, but you never wrote back."

Ernie stared at the letter he had just pulled from an envelope. "I never received these." He flipped over the envelope to the address. "Levinski…"

Natalie stepped in, "She only had Levinski's name from the music box so she mailed them there, but sir, why would Mr. Levinski keep these from you?"

Ernie shook his head and placed his wrinkled and burned hand over his mouth. "He found out."

"Found out what?" Ryan asked.

Ernie shook his head some more. "I told my father our family's corrupt actions would haunt him someday, but instead, they haunted me." Ernie stared at the front of the envelope and shook his head.

"You see, my grandfather and father stole most of the land we used for the peaches. Faulty contracts, lies, and deceit. Took the most from Levinski's family. When I learned about it, I couldn't bring myself to tell my best friend, so I just prayed he'd never find out. But he did and that explains a lot about things that had changed when I returned from war."

Natalie's mind raced back to the land deed she had seen at the Taylor House Museum. "The land deeds were wrong?" she asked.

Ernie looked at her and nodded. "Nearly every single one of them. But no one questioned it because my dad was paying the town so well at the time. People just let it slide, but after I returned from the war and the trains had officially stopped running, some people came to me wanting what was theirs. I didn't care. It was easy to shut them all out and eventually, they stopped coming. That is until Mayor Harrison arrived at my house asking about the station."

"That was because of me," said Ryan. "My mom left me this," he showed Ernie the ticket stub. "I thought if I could use the station as a set to the movie, I could find out more without drawing attention to who I was and what I wanted. I just needed time to figure everything out, but even I became too afraid and I just kept hitting dead ends. But somehow," Ryan nodded to Natalie and John Paul, "These two were able to do it."

"But we didn't!" said Natalie. "We lost it, sir. All your family's money that you hid at the station. It's all gone!"

Ernie patted Ryan's hand. "That money never meant anything to me the moment I lost my Charlotte. This is what matters," and he pulled Ryan's hand to his lips and gave it a kiss. "I wish I would have known that then."

@juliettecharles

Official account of Juliette Charles
May we bring only beauty into the world

Incredibly saddened by the tragic death of Guy Barnes, but excited to announce that his last movie will go on as planned in his memory.

Chapter 47

"I still can't believe Levinski got away," said John Paul as he hammered a nail into a piece of siding on the treehouse.

"You heard Officer Hughes. They have some good leads and hope to find him in the next week. He can't go far with all that money," said Natalie, handing him another piece of wood. "I just still can't believe you are a convicted criminal!"

"Hey, now! I told you, I am waiting on that conviction. If it all works out, my name will be cleared."

Once they had left the hospital room to let Ryan and Ernie reconnect, Natalie had pulled John Paul into a janitor's closet and had him explain his story. She had been so mad at him for not telling her, and she still wasn't letting it go.

"Vandalism! Of a food truck!" she laughed now about it.

"I told you I just bought the spray paint. I didn't know what the guys intended to use it for!"

"Right, because thirteen-year-old boys typically use spray paint for DIY projects!"

John Paul rolled his eyes at her. "Another board, please. We are almost finished with the final wall." Natalie decided to drop the tormenting for now as she handed him another piece of wood. She was amazed at how much progress they had made in just five days. Without spending their time trying to solve local mysteries, they had plenty of it to build the treehouse, and not to mention a perfect view of the movie set at the station below.

It was an easy call by the studio after all the press and fan attention from Juliette Charles' Instagram account to continue filming. She hit one million followers after sharing Natalie's rescue story. Then came the posts about the treasure, the long-lost reunion of a grandfather and grandson, and the discovery of the letters written by Addison West.

With Ryan's approval, the letters were made available to the public as they served as a full autobiography of the actress.

Natalie watched as the movie crew finished up their filming for the day. She spotted Ernie and Ryan stand up from their chairs. Ernie was saying something to Ryan and then he put his arm around his shoulder and led him to the back platform of the station. Ryan hopped down and then turned around to help Ernie. They walked along the train tracks together and into the sun's fading light.

"I guess they both found the treasure they had always wanted," John Paul said.

"Yeah," Natalie said with a smile. "It looks like they did."

Epilogue

Thursday, August 20

THE LOS ANGELES NEWS

Addison West Museum to Open in Berlin, Maryland

By Grayson Guilfoyle

What was once an old train station, and more recently a filming site for Juliette Charles' upcoming movie *Tracks*, has been converted into a museum to honor the life of actress Addison West. Throughout her career, this entertainment icon's private life was kept a secret, but since stories from her past were recently discovered by her son Ryan West with the help of two local kids from Berlin, Maryland, the world can now get a glimpse into the life of the actress they had loved so dearly.

With over a five hundred handwritten letters from Addison to her long-lost father, the museum takes you through the remarkable life of this woman, who proves through her writings that she was so much more than an actress.

The museum is set to open next Saturday, the 29th of August, with all proceeds going to support local businesses and farms in Berlin.

Acknowledgments

First and foremost, I would like to thank my husband, Jarrett. My best friend and biggest supporter. You were the one who first introduced me to the incredible town of Berlin, Maryland - your childhood home. You kept with me through it all. Your stories are my stories, and my stories are yours.

For Andrea Galdi and Kim Merola. Andrea, you were my first reader and had no idea what you were getting into when I approached you that day in the teacher's lounge, but your support, encouragement, and constant need for that next chapter kept me writing and believing I could do it. I will forever be grateful for this selfless act of kindness. Kim, you never doubted me and always told it to me straight.

For my niece Laura, you were my first dedicated young reader, and your critique meant the world.

For my dad, a red pen always in hand. You taught me to love everything about the written word, including all things grammar-related. I owe my love of (probably overused) commas to you. Thanks for being harsh enough to push me forward but caring enough to know I still needed at least one good critique.

Mom. My love of words always falls short when I think of how to explain all the love and appreciation I have for you and for all you do for me and your children and grandchildren. You are a saint, an angel, a giver, a hugger, but most importantly, a friend.

Thank you to my siblings. Nate, Aaron, Liz, and Andrew. You made life fun and filled my childhood with memories and stories.

Thanks to my brother-in-law, Vin. You may not remember but your advice first lit the match. On my birthday hike through the woods, I asked for your life coaching support and after some conversation, you said "Write the book." So here it is. I wrote the book.

Thank you to these incredible people from Berlin, Maryland. Allison Early, Carol Rose, Susan Taylor, Donna Main, Mayor Gee Williams, Cassandra Brown, and Ivy Wells. You all took the time to meet with a complete no-name author who simply had a dream of writing a book. I will never forget your kindness that day at the Calvin Taylor House Museum when you each shared your love for your town and helped inspire this story.

Lastly, thank you to my readers, the young and young at heart. You make books what they are — a true source of magic.

About the Author

Maria Grosskettler is a lover of the written word. She knows the power and magic it holds. As an elementary teacher, she strives to inspire this same love into young readers and writers. As a writer, she strives to bring that magic into the hands and minds of readers, both young and young at heart.

When not reading, writing, or teaching, Maria enjoys spending time with her husband and son, seeking adventures every day. As a family, they enjoy traveling, hiking, biking, and kayaking. She lives in Maryland but spends as much time as she can traveling the world, creating her own stories.

Made in the USA
Middletown, DE
12 August 2021